John Creasey – Master Storyteller

Born in Surrey, England in 1908 into a poor family in which there were nine children, John Creasey grew up to be a true master story teller and international sensation. His more than 600 crime, mystery and thriller titles have now sold 80 million copies in 25 languages. These include many popular series such as *Gideon of Scotland Yard*, *The Toff*, *Dr Palfrey* and *The Baron*.

Creasy wrote under many pseudonyms, explaining that booksellers had complained he totally dominated the 'C' section in stores. They included:

Gordon Ashe, M E Cooke, Norman Deane, Robert Caine Frazer, Patrick Gill, Michael Halliday, Charles Hogarth, Brian Hope, Colin Hughes, Kyle Hunt, Abel Mann, Peter Manton, J J Marric, Richard Martin, Rodney Mattheson, Anthony Morton and Jeremy York.

Never one to sit still, Creasey had a strong social conscience, and stood for Parliament several times, along with founding the One Party Alliance which promoted the idea of government by a coalition of the best minds from across the political spectrum.

He also founded the British Crime Writers' Association, which to this day celebrates outstanding crime writing. The Mystery Writers of America bestowed upon him the Edgar Award for best novel and then in 1969 the ultimate Grand Master Award. John Creasey's stories are as compelling today as ever.

THE TOFF SERIES

The Toff
Takes Shares

John Creasey

HOUSE OF
STRATUS

This edition published in 2012 by House of Stratus, an imprint of
Stratus Books Ltd., Lisandra House, Fore Street,
Looe, Cornwall, PL13 1AD, U.K.
www.houseofstratus.com

Typeset by House of Stratus.

A catalogue record for this book is available from the British Library
and the Library of Congress.

ISBN 07551-3672-1
EAN 978-07551-3672-8

Chapter One

The Resourceful Lady

A car was travelling towards him, and Rollison slowed down again and dipped his headlights. The light from the other car made him narrow his eyes. He turned the driving-mirror a little, so that he could see the back of the Rolls. He saw nothing but his cases. Perhaps he had imagined a sneeze!

The other car passed. The wind had dropped and the only sound was the purring of the engine. The road ahead was clear.

Rollison looked straight ahead of him, and said: "Good evening."

There was no answer.

"Aren't you rather cramped back there?" asked Rollison.

There was no sound.

"I think you must be," persisted Rollison, cheerfully, "and when another sneezing fit seizes you, it'll be much better to be able to let it come. Don't you agree?"

There was a cautious movement behind him.

"That's much better," he said. "I've no particular objection to giving you a lift, you know, but I'd like to see my passenger. Shall I stop?"

The movement had not been intentional; there was still no response. His smile faded; it might be a dog, caught sleeping in the car. He pulled into the side of the road and stopped. He turned – and a woman's head appeared above the back seat. The only light was the reflection from the headlamps, but he could see a mop of dark hair and a pale face. He switched on the roof light. It seemed very bright, and made the woman blink; she was very young. She had blue eyes and a pale, heart-shaped face; and Rollison no longer wondered what had happened to the girl who had been asking for him.

"Oh," he said. "Hallo!"

The girl sniffed, and fumbled in her bag. Rollison took a handkerchief from his pocket, flapped it open and held it out to her.

"Thanks," she murmured. She took and used it vigorously, and then sat down on the seat immediately behind him.

"Now why not come in the front with me?" asked Rollison.

She stared at him uncertainly.

She put out her hand to touch the handle, and Rollison got out of the car hurriedly. He winced when he caught his bruised leg on the door, but had the back door open before she had moved, and helped her out.

She bent down and rubbed her leg.

"Cramp?" suggested Rollison.

"Just—just a bit," she admitted.

She straightened up and walked about the grass verge. A little stream of cars passed, and in the headlights her face showed more clearly. She was flushed with embarrassment, and the blueness of her eyes had to be seen to be believed. She had a good complexion, too. She was dressed in a simple dark suit and stood little higher than Rollison's shoulder.

"Ready?" he asked, opening the door.

"Yes, thank you." She was still nervous, which was not surprising, and gave him a quick, shy glance as she got into the car. He went round to the other side, took the wheel, and offered her a cigarette. She accepted eagerly. He started off, and for ten minutes neither of them said a word. His manner was mystifying her and it seemed to Rollison that the more he puzzled her, the more freely and more quickly she would talk.

Rollison broke the silence after a long time.

"Are you coming all the way to London?"

"Yes, please," she said.

Did she intend to offer no explanation until he questioned her in earnest? Or was she still so nervous that she could not find words? He began to talk – about the weather, the match that afternoon, trifles which won from her an occasional remark and once a quick, flashing smile; he saw that in the dashboard lights, which he had kept on deliberately. He liked this stranger, and the mystery heightened his interest.

They passed through Amesbury.

"That's a stage of the journey over," said Rollison. "With luck we'll be in London before one o'clock. What part do you live?"

"The West End," she said.

"Near me?"

"Not very far away," said the girl, and stared at him for what seemed a long time. Then she volunteered timidly: "You're very good."

"Just interested," said Rollison. "You were asking for me at the inn, weren't you?"

"Yes. I—I was anxious to talk to you."

"You've three hours ahead of you, with no one else to talk to," encouraged Rollison.

"I don't know where to start."

"Try the middle," said Rollison. "We can go back to the beginning afterwards, if you feel like it. Or try at the end, if you prefer to," he went on helpfully. "It's useful to work backwards sometimes. The end seems to be what you wanted to talk to me about so badly that you followed me from London to Somerset, plucked up courage and then lost it, and decided to stow away."

She laughed.

"I suppose that *does* sum it up, but I didn't come from London to see you. I had to come down in any case. Then I saw that you were playing at Taunton this afternoon, and I came along and watched."

"Was it a good game to watch?"

"I don't know much about Rugby," she said, "but it was *fast*. Did you get badly hurt?"

"Nothing that a day or two's rest won't put right," said Rollison. "What happened after you'd been to the match?"

"Well—I found out where the team was going to stay tonight."

"Good detective work!"

"Not really. I asked one of the stewards and he asked someone else, and told me. I travelled on by train and got there just before you arrived."

"What put you off, once you were on the spot?"

She gave her quick, nervous laugh again.

"I asked one or two of the players for you, and—" she paused. "They grinned at each other, and it just made me feel I couldn't come and talk to you."

"I can imagine what it felt like," said Rollison feelingly. "They mean well, you know."

"Oh, I know. Peter's very much the same."

'Peter', thought Rollison, and he no longer wondered what the girl had come to talk about: Peter Lund, of course. He had no idea who she was. Peter had a reputation for being everyone's friend and nobody's darling, but it would be too much of a coincidence if she were talking about a different Peter.

"Peter who?" he asked.

"Peter Lund. My cousin."

"So you know Peter Lund," said Rollison, somewhat inanely.

She took the question seriously.

"Not really well. I'm younger than he is, and I haven't seen much of him since he came out of the R.A.F., you know. We've met once or twice, that's all. Before the war when he wasn't serious about anything, he often went on cricket tours—that's how you met him, isn't it?"

"Yes."

"He and the others were much the same as the crowd at the inn," said the girl, now talking with much greater freedom, "but I was in pigtails then, and I could take it."

"Shyness isn't reckoned a modern virtue," remarked Rollison.

"No. I felt like a fool, but—well, I've led rather a secluded life for the last few years. I wish I hadn't in some ways, but—oh, *that* doesn't matter."

"I think it does," said Rollison. "It all helps to show me the background. What kind of a secluded life?"

"I've been ill," she told him.

"Oh, I'm sorry."

"I'm better now," she assured him, "and the doctors tell me that I've nothing more to worry about. Living in a sanatorium for years doesn't broaden the mind very much, you know, and—well, it's all rather strange. I hardly recognised Peter. He seems to have grown so much older than I have."

"The R.A.F. did that to a lot of people," said Rollison.

"Yes, I know," She looked up at him, and smiled faintly. "I wasn't cut right off from the world, you know; I read the newspapers. A little about Peter, when he won his D.F.C., and a lot about you when—"

"I failed to win anything!"

She laughed.

"I read the *London Gazette,* too. Mr. Rollison, I'm quite sure that if anyone can help Peter, it's you. If you will, that is. I know he wants you to."

"We have talked about it." said Rollison.

"I know. But he—" She hesitated, and looked about her as if again at a loss for words. Rollison handed her his cigarette-case, and she took a cigarette gratefully. She shielded the light of the flame, so as not to dazzle him.

"Thanks," she said. "Have you seen much of Peter lately?"

"Not very much. I didn't think it wise."

"Why not?"

"People are apt to think odd things if I show myself too often," said Rollison lightly. "Peter thinks he has cause for suspicion. If he has, he's probably watched fairly closely, and to be seen too often with me might precipitate events. I don't think we want that."

Deliberately he had been rather vague. She sat smoking, thinking it out. Then she nodded, and looked up at him.

"I see what you mean. So you *are* going to help him?"

"If I can."

"I'm sure you can," she said, and smiled freely. "It's a great relief! When you came away on this tour, Peter thought it meant that you thought he was talking out of the back of his neck. I've never seen anyone so depressed. He got drunk."

"Not very original," said Rollison lightly.

"It's unusual for Peter, I think. He was never a heavy drinker. He – and I know a lot about him from his mother, you know – he started to drink too heavily a few weeks ago. Not regularly, if you see what I mean, but in bouts. Something seemed to weigh on his mind and the only way he could get release from it was to drink until he forgot. That's not like Peter."

"It certainly isn't," agreed Rollison.

He felt annoyed with himself. He should have known that Peter had developed a tendency to drink too much, but it was news to him. He looked down at the dark hair and saw the tip of the girl's nose. He did not even know her name, but he did know that she was taking this thing very seriously. He wanted her to go on without being prompted, and when she had half finished her cigarette site began to talk again.

"Perhaps I'd better start at the beginning now! I didn't know anything about this—this worry, until I went to my aunt's to spend the night last week. Peter came in late, and absolutely helpless. Thank heavens Aunt had gone to bed! Thomas – that's the butler – helped Peter to get to bed, and I went to see him afterwards. He was talking wildly about being frightened – he didn't actually use the word 'frightened' – but that's what it amounted to. He mentioned you. He said he'd been relying on you and you had gone off on this football tour, which showed that you weren't interested. You thought he was dreaming; no one believed him, and he confided in no one else. He was like that," went on the girl soberly. "He contradicted himself every minute or two, but some things emerged quite clearly, and one of them was that he was depending on you for help. I had to go to Bath – that's where I stayed in the sanatorium – and it wasn't very far out of my way to come to Taunton to see you. Then your friends rather put me off, and I thought if I hid in the car—When you discovered me I was in a panic," the girl confessed.

"I just couldn't speak. I don't think you would have found me so soon, but the cases fell on me when you stopped, and I sneezed. I'd been trying not to for ages. The cases made me lose my control and out it came."

"We aren't going to complain about that," said Rollison. "So Peter's so worried that he gets drunk and you thought you would put a word in. That was nice of you."

"Well, I had to try," said the girl. "You see, something happened which made me realise that Peter wasn't talking out of the back of his neck. I thought he was frightened, and now I know he had reason to be. I felt sure that if I could convince you of that you would help him."

After a long pause, Rollison asked quietly: "What makes you feel so sure that he's got reason to be scared?"

The girl said: "I wonder if you *will* believe me? It's so—odd. Almost fantastic. It was something which happened on Saturday …"

Chapter Two

Reason For Fear

"A man stopped me in the street," the girl said, and paused.

Rollison made no comment. Two cyclists, riding well on the crown of the road, forced him to pull over to the side. He did not think the girl noticed them, so great an impression had her encounter made on her.

"I'd never seen him before," she went on in a low-pitched voice. "I'm not sure that I would recognise him again, he was—just a man. He was rather shabbily dressed, and he spoke in a hoarse voice. He startled me because he called me by name. '*Miss Hellier*,' he called, and I stopped short."

The 'Miss Hellier' came out in a husky voice, as if she were imitating the voice of the man who had accosted her.

"He took my arm and led me into a shop doorway," went on the girl. "I don't know why, but I was scared even then. It wasn't the man, he wasn't frightening, he was so ordinary. He looked at me rather oddly, and then asked me whether I had seen my cousin Peter lately. I thought he might be an acquaintance of Peter's—Peter always made such queer friends, you know."

"Yes," said Rollison.

"So I told him I had. Then he made it dear that he knew I had *and* knew that Peter had been drunk. He asked me whether he had talked about anything special, and I said 'No.' I was getting more frightened by then, but it was in the street and people were passing all the time and I didn't think there was anything really to worry about. So I let him talk. It took him a long time to reach the point—and the point he was so anxious to make was that if Peter had told me anything I wasn't to speak to anyone about it. He said that Peter had a lot of queer ideas; that he'd been smashed up badly during the war and imagined things; and he kept repeating the same question—had Peter told me anything? I asked him what kind of thing, and he said I'd know if Peter had mentioned it. I just acted dumb," went on the girl. "It seemed the only thing to do. All Peter had told me was that he was worried and nervous and that he had asked you for help and thought you were letting him down. Well, I satisfied the fellow, I think, and he went off. I finished my shopping and went on to my friends. All the time I kept thinking about you. Then I looked in the newspaper and happened to catch sight of a paragraph about you touring with the Norfolk side, so—here I am. You must believe me, please. It's gospel truth."

"I'm sure it is," said Rollison.

"And you'll help Peter?"

Rollison said: "I'm going back to see him now. My man telephoned me and told me he thought that would be useful."

The girl drew in her breath.

"Nothing's happened to Peter?"

"No, or I should have been told."

"Oh," she said. "I—I'm glad you're helping."

"You haven't thought of going to the police?" murmured Rollison.

"Of course not!" She sounded alarmed. "Peter was so anxious that the police shouldn't know anything about it. He didn't make many things clear, but he was definite about that. That's one of the reasons why I'm worried. Peter's had a strange life, you know."

Rollison chuckled.

"I don't think you need fear that he's being blackmailed, or that he's got anything on his conscience."

"But he *is* frightened."

"Of what's going to happen, not of what has happened," Rollison assured her.

He was tempted to tell her how much he knew, including the fact that Peter was worried about Majors. One thing deterred him – the fact that she had been accosted. She might have been followed since. It was possible that she had been followed as far as the inn, and that it was known that she had come to see him. If she were approached again it might be harmful if she were in a position to give away much information. He nursed his thoughts, talking reassuringly as he did so. Peter's worries he dismissed vaguely as 'business troubles'. Did the girl know much about his work?

"Only what his mother told me," said Miss Hellier.

That had been a fair summary of Peter's recent activities.

He had come out of the R.A.F. with no clear notion of what he was going to do, and had gone into Majors because his father had been a director. He had not expected to stay long; office life held no attractions for Peter, who had been a wanderer before the war; a man who looked for trouble and often found it, who had travelled over most of the globe and had a nodding acquaintance with many countries. Above all things he had enjoyed life.

After a few weeks at Majors he had discovered that he had a flair for publicity.

Majors was not one of London's biggest or most exclusive stores. It was neither another Harrods nor another Selfridges, but imitated them both.

Then Peter had discovered his flair – or, perhaps more truthfully, Augustus Romeo had discovered it for him.

Augustus Romeo was a remarkable man.

For years a member of Majors' board, he had been in the United States on a buying mission at the outbreak of war, and he had succeeded in attaching himself to one of the Government buying missions and had stayed for a long time in the States. In London he had been almost forgotten, although before the war he had been a colourful personality, renowned for shock tactics on the Stock Exchange. The Exchange had not viewed him with a friendly eye, disliking shock tactics, but had he stayed for a few years there was little doubt that he would have made his mark. Socially, he was tolerated; and socially, he had made it clear, he intended to make an even greater mark. In appearance Romeo was a big, handsome man with the air of an actor who had a great opinion of himself. His booming voice had a mellow quality; most certainly he had a way with him.

Soon after his return he had become managing director of Majors, and had promptly announced his intention of making it *the* London store. Publicity, he had claimed, was the secret of success – publicity first and last and everywhere between. What Majors lacked was intelligent – no, brilliant! – publicity. And Romeo had discovered a flair for publicity in Peter Lund.

So far, so good.

There was much to be said for Peter's publicity. Majors became more widely known. People who had regarded it as a suburban store on the fringes of the West End began to change their minds. Yet in spite of that Majors' shares fell; perhaps it was because the market distrusted Romeo, although Romeo had never given any known cause for distrust.

Peter thought that someone on the board was responsible. There were too many staff changes. The standard of service fell abruptly at a time when it should have risen. No, Peter was not at all happy. He thought that someone was trying to make a racket out of Majors. He did not think that Romeo was responsible; that might have been because he had good reason to be grateful to the flamboyant man home from America. There *was* trouble; and Rollison had looked for the source of it but had failed to find any evidence until the girl told him of her encounter.

She was sleeping with her chin on her chest, and breathing rather heavily. Her head kept falling against Rollison's shoulder. After a while, he let it rest there. The road was clear, and he could move her if he needed more freedom of action. His left leg was aching, and his eye was painful from the strain of driving; he could have done with more beef steak. He smiled to himself when he thought of the party at the inn.

In the driving-mirror he saw the light of a car behind him.

He had passed very few on the road, and none which had not dropped out almost at once. This car had turned on to the road a few yards behind him, and had fallen back a little way and then followed. The driver might like driving on another man's headlights; that was the reasonable thing to suppose, but Rollison felt a little uneasy. He could not get the thought of a little nondescript man out of his mind – a man who had frightened the girl so much that she had dared to venture so far.

The car behind kept its distance.

The girl's head was heavy against his arm.

He did not want to wake her, but he wanted to find out what the other driver was doing. He drove up a hill. His headlights shone on a tree-lined road, almost an avenue of trees, in front of him. It looked eerie in the lights, dark branches gradually fading into darkness outside the range of the beams. He remembered that the trees continued on either side for the better part of a mile.

He felt uneasy as he went into it.

Reflected light came back from the trees as they flashed by. The other car was still close behind. Rollison put on more speed; if anything were going to happen it would be better to be clear of the trees. He was half-way along the avenue when the other car put on an impressive spurt and passed him; almost at once it pulled across his path and slowed down. He jammed on his brakes, and the girl sat up abruptly.

Chapter Three

Encounters

"What is it?" gasped the girl.

"It's all right," Rollison reassured her.

He could swing the wheel and get past the car in front, but he chose to stop the engine. The driver of the leading car was getting out. He was a young fellow, wearing yellow gloves which were caught in the glare of the headlights. His dark hair was brushed smoothly down, and he was smiling. He looked debonair in well-cut clothes, and raised a hand as if in greeting.

"Good evening," said Rollison heavily.

The girl was sitting stiff and upright now, staring towards the stranger, who drew level with the driving-window and leaned against it.

"Hallo, hallo!" he greeted. "I'm sorry if I pulled across your bows. I judged it badly, I'm afraid."

"Very badly," agreed Rollison.

"You don't sound as if you've forgiven me," said the stranger, who was much too self-assured. He peered first at Rollison and then at the girl, giving her a long, protracted stare. "And all I want is a light," he added brightly.

"A light?"

A cigarette appeared in the man's fingers.

"I've been longing for a cigarette for the last half-hour, and couldn't last out any longer."

Rollison took out his lighter and flicked it. The man's face was clearly visible in the flame; he was good-looking in a bold way, and his gaze strayed towards the girl again as he drew on the cigarette.

"Ah, thanks! I'll have to chain-smoke all the way to town."

"Don't do that," said Rollison. He took a packet of book-matches from his pocket and handed it to the motorist.

"So I am forgiven! Thanks!"

"Next time you pull across me like that I shall probably dent your back panel," said Rollison.

"Let's hope there isn't a next time," returned the other. "Lashings of thanks. Good night!" He took the cigarette from his lips and waved his hand; the glowing end made a circle of red as he turned and made off.

Rollison let him drive away first. Then he followed slowly. The red light slowly faded and soon disappeared completely.

"There's some power in that engine," Rollison mused aloud.

"What—what did he want?" asked the girl.

"A light," said Rollison.

"Do you really believe that?"

Her flat was in Ellerby Mews, not five minutes' drive from his own in Gresham Terrace. He started to get out of the car, to see her to her door, but she firmly refused to let him do that. The headlights shone on a flight of wooden steps and the door of the garage over which she lived. The steps creaked as she went up them. He backed out of the mews as she opened and closed the front door.

Something moved in the shadows.

Rollison made the engine hum as he backed into the main street, then quietened it, drove a few yards, stopped and jumped out. He hurried back to the entrance to the mews. It was pitch dark, but the rain had stopped. The wind was not strong, but now and again a gust almost lifted his hat from his head. He stood at one corner, peering towards the flat. He saw a light at a window, showing that an inside light was on. He saw the girl moving about, then saw the figure of a man move across the lighted square of the window.

He heard no sound.

He crept forward, remembering the creaking noise which the steps had made. He would not be able to get up them without warning whoever was there, but there seemed no way for the man to escape. As he drew nearer, he heard a scratching sound; the man was picking the lock of the front door.

The light went out, leaving him in utter darkness.

The faint noise came across the darkness, holding an eerie note. So the marauder was still there. Soon he was able to discern the outline of the man's figure.

The scratching sound stopped.

Although everything was silent, Rollison was sure that the door had opened. He went up quickly; the creaking was not loud. He reached the door and, peering inside, saw a faint glow of light. The man who had forced entry was half-way across a small hall.

Rollison stood in the doorway.

As he grew accustomed to the dim light he could see the man's outline, with a hand at his coat pocket; that might mean that the marauder held a gun. There were faint sounds from the inner room followed by a whisper of voices; two girls were talking. The man by the door kept his right hand near his pocket and stretched forward to touch the handle with his left.

Another door closed as two girls said, "Good night."

The man opened the inner door.

He seemed to know where he was going as he moved towards the right. Three doors were just visible in the faint light coming from the top and sides of one of them – presumably the door of the room into which Miss Hellier had just gone. The intruder went softly towards it and turned the handle. He drew his right hand from his pocket, but Rollison was still not sure what he held.

The light grew better as the door opened more widely. It shone on the man's hand and a gun.

Rollison stepped forward swiftly, making no attempt to keep quiet. The man swung round; the girl gasped. Rollison could not see her, and just then he was interested only in the man. He struck out at the gun, but he was a shade too late; a shot rang out and there was a bright flash. Rollison felt the wind of the bullet near his head. He drove a clenched fist into the man's face as the girl from the other room screamed out.

Peter Lund's cousin made no sound. Rollison could see her shadow against the door, with her hands upraised.

The man did not speak, simply flung out his arm and tried to knock Rollison aside. Rollison struck at the gun-arm. The gun fell to the floor, the man drew back. Then a bright light came on, and Rollison could see everything more clearly.

The man in front of him was the debonair fellow from the other car. He no longer looked handsome; ugly he was now, with fear and desperation. He struck out savagely, and Rollison dodged the blow and at the same time kicked the gun out of reach.

"Pick that up. Hurry!" He called to the girl.

The man launched himself forward. Rollison tried to fend him off, but caught a heavy blow on the side of the head. The man rushed across the hall towards the front door, while Miss Hellier's friend stood rooted in the doorway of her room, arms upraised, a scream stifled on her lips. If she had moved she could have tripped the man up, but he reached the outer door, and sprang outside. He jumped from the landing to the ground, avoiding the steps.

Rollison went after him, but stopped on the landing.

The light shining from the flat shone on the man as he reached the ground and turned and ran towards the exit of the mews. He was soon lost to sight. His footsteps rang on the pavement, and there was another sound, like an echo, but heavier.

Two men were running.

The light shone on a policeman's helmet. The policeman passed the end of the mews swiftly, intent on catching the obvious fugitive. Rollison turned from the landing outside the door.

Peter's cousin was coming forward with a macintosh clutched at her waist.

"Put out that light," called Rollison.

She turned round and obeyed. When the light went out there was only a dim glow from the inner rooms. Rollison went in and closed the door, and as he did so the other girl, who was still standing in the doorway, swayed and gasped: "Alice—Alice, what was it? What—"

"It's all right, dear," said Alice Hellier quickly. "It's all right now; this is a friend. It's all right," repeated Alice. "Don't worry."

"What—what's that you've got in your hand? It's a gun!" The other girl was almost screaming now.

Rollison took the gun from Peter's cousin, and Alice turned and led the other girl into the bedroom. The door closed.

Rollison wrapped the gun in a handkerchief, slipped it into his pocket and lit a cigarette. All the time he listened intently for any sound from outside; he heard none.

Both girls were talking, the unknown in a high-pitched voice not far removed from hysterical. Alice was soothing her; that girl had her wits about her.

Rollison did not know whether the policeman had noticed the flat from which the light had been coming. If so, he would soon be here to make inquiries. Rollison hoped he would not come. Then he heard a man plodding past, and imagined that the policeman was returning to his beat.

Alice came out of the bedroom.

"Will you—will you have a word with her?" she asked, in a subdued voice. "She's still so frightened. You might be able to calm her down."

"I'll try," agreed Rollison. "Just a moment."

The plodding footsteps passed, so there was no immediate likelihood of an inquiry from the patrol policeman.

Rollison went into a pleasantly furnished bedroom. The other girl was blonde; pretty but neurotic, thought Rollison. Her lips were parted and she was struggling for breath.

Alice said something about making tea, and disappeared.

Rollison sat on the edge of the bed; the last thing he wanted to do just then was to soothe this girl; there were so many pressing matters; but he had to try to quieten her. He was a friend of Alice's he assured her; he had driven Alice home and seen the burglar. *"Burglar!"*

"Yes, there are too many of them about," said Rollison easily.

"Then—then the *police!*" Well, no harm had been done, said Rollison, and by bringing the police in it would mean newspaper headlines, and—

"No, no!" cried the girl. "No, not that!"

"Then we'll have to try to avoid it," said Rollison. He lit a cigarette and gave it to her, and the first draw made her choke. After a while she grew calmer, and when Alice came in with tea she smiled a little shamefacedly.

Obviously Peter's cousin had heard the talk of burglars and had no intention of disclosing the truth – or the apparent truth, that the man of the road had come here and had lain in wait.

For what?

For murder …

"Yes, I'll be all right now," the fair-haired girl was saying. "I *am* sorry I made such a fool of myself. That shot!" She shivered and looked in distress at Rollison, who laughed and told her he had been just as scared himself.

"You—you don't think they'll come again, do you?"

"I think this is the last place they'd try again," soothed Rollison; "they'll expect the police to be in charge. I'll see that there's nothing to worry about. Good night."

"Good night."

Rollison went out. Alice followed him, leaving the door ajar. Without speaking, she nodded towards her room, and Rollison preceded her. Seeing a telephone by the side of her bed, he went to it and dialled the number of his Gresham Terrace flat, without speaking to Alice. He was answered so promptly that he knew that his man had not been in bed.

"Hallo, Jolly."

"I hope you've had no trouble on the road, sir," said Jolly.

"Nothing serious. Are you fit for night duty?"

"Quite fit, sir," said Jolly promptly.

"Then come round to Ellerby Mews at once," said Rollison. "The number is—" he paused, and looked at Alice.

"Three," she said.

"Three," echoed Rollison. "Before you leave, give Snub a ring and ask him to be at the flat as soon as he can."

"He's staying here," said Jolly.

"Good. I'll see you here—at the mews."

Rollison replaced the receiver and smiled at Alice. She had taken off her dress before the incident, and her bare legs showed beneath the macintosh. Her hair was untidy and she looked tired, but there was radiance in her smile when she returned his gaze.

"*Thank* you," she said.

Rollison shrugged his shoulders.

"I'm glad to help," he murmured. "It's getting rather stickier than I hoped."

"It doesn't matter so much now that you're helping," she said, and then added in a lower voice, "It was the man who stopped and asked for a light, wasn't it?"

"Yes," said Rollison.

"I *think* he works at Majors," said Alice Hellier.

Chapter Four

A Story For The Police

"Now that's being helpful," smiled Rollison. He sat on the edge, of her bed. "It's time that we began to ask ourselves what we're doing," he added. "The police don't know where the trouble was, but the policeman who passed probably heard the shot and will certainly know there was trouble. He might make inquiries. Peter's anxious that the police shouldn't hear of anything yet, isn't he?"

"He was," said Alice. "I know so little about it." Her clear, blue eyes seemed to grow large and round. "Do you think we ought to tell them?"

"Yes."

"Then we'd better," she said, and drew in her breath. "But don't you want to know why you were sent for first? I mean, if there's no *need* to tell the police—"

"Alice," said Rollison, and paused.

She waited.

"The man came here to kill you, you know."

"I'm not worried about the danger," she declared, and gave a little laugh. "I can't understand all this, that's the trouble. It must be something very—serious."

"Yes," said Rollison dryly.

She raised her hands.

"Well, I'll have to leave everything to you. Peter is prepared to, and that's good enough for me. You will see that everything's all right tonight, won't you?"

"My man will be on duty outside until daybreak," Rollison promised. "But I don't expect more trouble, they'll assume that the place will be guarded. You must be very careful where you go for the next few days, though. Will you let me or my man know where you're likely to go?"

"If it will help, yes."

"Don't forget," warned Rollison. "Good night."

She came to the door with him, still expressing her thanks, then went back to her room. He stood in the breeze, hat in hand, still puzzled by her remarkable composure. She had been much more worried about talking to him in the car than she had been by the danger to herself.

He heard two policemen talking as they walked past the mews entrance, but they did not turn into it. Had he been right earlier when he had thought a policeman passed the little flat? He was turning that over in his mind and trying to decide on the wisest course of action when a man turned into the mews. He could not see him clearly until the new-comer was close at hand, when a familiar voice said: "Is that you, sir?"

"Ah, Jolly! Welcome."

"Thank you, sir."

"Three things," said Rollison quickly. "There's been an attack on Mr. Lund's cousin, who lives here. If the police come the official story is burglars, and that I was at hand and asked you to keep guard here. All right?"

"Perfectly clear, sir," said Jolly.

"Good. And the third thing—what happened to make you send for me?"

"The crisis which I thought was developing passed off," said Jolly primly, "but I think it well that you're here, sir. The initial cause of my anxiety was Mr. Lund, who arrived at the flat—er—somewhat the worse for drink."

"Oh," said Rollison, "did he?"

"He was in a considerable state of alarm, and thought he had been followed and was in personal danger," said Jolly, as if he were reading from a careful statement. "I telephoned you when I had seen that a man was standing outside the flat. After the conversation with you I went out, and the man moved off. Mr. Higginhottom is now looking after Mr. Lund, who is—ah—sleeping it off."

"And he's all right?"

"Except for the customary symptoms, yes, sir."

"Do the police know anything?"

"I have left it to you to tell the police if you think it necessary, sir."

"Good," said Rollison. "Just keep an eye on things here. I'll see that you're relieved in the morning."

Rollison smiled, patted his arm and left him.

The car was still parked in the road at the end of the mews, and he was not surprised when a figure loomed out of the darkness as he took the wheel. The sidelights were strong enough to show a policeman; the man had noticed the car and undoubtedly had connected it with the fleeing fugitive.

"Good morning," said Rollison.

"Good morning, sir." The man's voice was flat. "May I see your driving licence, please?"

"Why, yes. Burglars about?" asked Rollison, taking out his wallet.

"Just a check-up, sir, thank you." The man studied it and then looked keenly at Rollison. "Mr. *Rollison*—thank you, sir. What time did you leave the car here?"

"About a quarter to one."

"I see, sir. Thank you. I'm sorry to have worried you," added the policeman, and Rollison wished him good morning and drove off.

He had no doubt that this would be reported and that he would be questioned about it again; he would have good time to decide what to do by then. He was in a cheerful if puzzled frame of mind as he drove to the flat.

He left the car in the street; the policeman on duty there would not make a fuss about it, and he might need it again in a hurry. He went upstairs, and the front door of his flat was opened by a young man with a merry, smiling face, a mop of unruly hair and a snub nose.

This was Higginbottom, his secretary.

Higginbottom had been dubbed Snub on their first meeting, and had remained Snub, except to Jolly, who preferred to be formal. The secretary and the general factotum worked well together and respected each other, and many of Rollison's labours were consequently lightened.

"Hallo, hallo!" greeted Snub, standing aside to let him enter. "So you've deserted the young hooligans who were trying to break your neck, and—Oh-oh! What's happened to your eye?"

"Too little beef steak," said Rollison.

"That's what hasn't happened to it," retorted Snub. He closed the door and Rollison led the way to the living-room. He sat on the corner of his desk, and Snub looked at him with eyes which were brimming over with good humour. "Sorry if I'm a bit lighthearted," went on Snub. "I have a feeling that excitement has entered our drab lives again; you wouldn't have come back if you hadn't expected something pyrotechnical. What's this about a cousin of Peter Lund's?"

"Young and charming."

"The dog! He's never mentioned her."

"How is Peter?" asked Rollison.

"In a shocking state! I've seen some people blotto, but nothing quite like this before. Absolutely flat. Apparently he came round in a state of what Jolly calls agitation and delivered himself of the causes thereof, and then he went out. I look in every ten minutes or so, because as a sight it's unique. Nothing much has happened here since Jolly frightened off a customer who seemed to be showing some interest in our Peter. What's afoot?"

Rollison told him briefly.

Snub listened eagerly, and when it was finished turned to the door and said: "After that you want some coffee. Jolly left it on. Or would you rather have tea?" he called from the hall.

"Coffee, thanks."

"Okay!" Snub clattered crockery in the kitchen, and there followed a brief period of silence. It was broken by a harsh sawing sound, which startled Rollison until he realised that it was Peter's snoring. He went to the door of the spare bedroom and looked in.

Peter was lying on his back, with his mouth wide open. He was not a pretty sight. They had undressed him as far as his shirt, which was open at the neck, and the bedclothes had been roughly pulled over him. His hair was on end and his face, never a handsome one, looked almost grotesquely ugly. Rollison remembered the stories of Peter's deeds; and he saw, in place of that wide-open mouth and screwed-up eyes, a personable youngster, tight-lipped, staring with far-seeing eyes into the impenetrable blue of the heavens.

Peter turned on his side and stopped snoring.

"You wouldn't believe it if you hadn't seen it for yourself, would you?" asked Snub, peering in.

Rollison smiled and closed the door. Snub went ahead with the coffee, and some sandwiches which he had also produced. He poured out and then looked up with a shrewd gleam in his eyes.

"What about the police?"

"We can't keep it from them indefinitely," said Rollison.

"Er—do you mind a suggestion?"

"Go ahead," encouraged Rollison,

Snub did not do so immediately, but turned and looked at one of the long walls of the room. It was adorned with a remarkable miscellany; there was a top hat which had been pierced by a bullet, a bunch of chicken's feathers stuck to some paper, several different kinds of automatics and knives – in fact an amazing variety, some of which were obviously connected with crime, others which looked innocuous.

"Every time I start to make suggestions I take a look at that wall and call myself a conceited ape," declared Snub. "I wonder what souvenir you'll pick up from this show. It's a pity you can't capture a snore or two and make a record of 'em!" He went on in much the same voice, although he became serious: "Why not have a word in Grice's ear? It needn't be official, but it will let you out if serious misdeeds came about. I mean, leave it to Grice whether he takes official action or not."

Rollison glanced at his watch. "It's too late to ring him now. We'll get some sleep. I want you to go along to relieve Jolly at about five o'clock."

"I'll shake down on the couch, shall I?"

"Turn into Jolly's room," said Rollison.

"I'll want a docket with permission signed by the boss," grinned Snub.

Rollison went into his room and inspected himself in the mirror. His eye was much more discoloured and swollen now. He undressed and bathed his eye gingerly, then examined his bruised leg. He rubbed embrocation in, yawning as he massaged.

Rollison got into bed and switched off the light.

Peter would have recovered enough by the afternoon to talk seriously, and much might come from that. Rollison yawned again and then tried to stop thinking. He must be up by eight o'clock and it was now past two. *Eight o'clock, eight o'clock, eight o'clock …*

He felt someone shake his shoulder gently.

"It is eight o'clock, sir," said Jolly.

"Oh!" exclaimed Rcllison, struggling up. Jolly looked fresh and rested. "You wear well," Rollison went on, "astonishingly well. Congratulations."

"Thank you, sir," said Jolly, pouring out tea.

"All quiet during the night?"

"No alarms at all, sir," said Jolly. "The only matter worth reporting is that the police showed an interest in Ellerby Mews and were watching it this morning at daybreak. Mr. Higginbottom concealed himself from them, but he might be approached now. He will give your name if he is, sir."

"That's all right," said Rollison. "Is Mr. Lund awake?"

"I haven't disturbed him, but he is sleeping much more naturally. I don't think it will hurt to wake him."

"I'll bath and shave first," said Rollison.

"And if I may, I will give a little attention to your eye," said Jolly, with a touch of severity.

At a quarter to nine Rollison went into Peter's room, carrying a tray of tea. Peter stirred. His mouth was closed but his hair was still rumpled and he badly needed a shave. Rollison put down the tray, sat on the edge of the bed, and touched Peter's shoulder.

Peter stiffened.

"Hallo, Peter," said Rollison.

The younger man relaxed and opened his eyes. He blinked, then licked his lips and made a wry face.

"Gosh! I feel terrible!"

"Have some tea," said Rollison, pouring some into a cup.

"Ah. Thanks." Peter struggled up and held out his hand for the cup. His eyes were bloodshot and his face haggard. He put a hand to his head and muttered to himself, then sipped the tea cautiously. He did not speak for several minutes; then for the first time he gave something like a smile and said, "My, what an eye!"

"Better an eye than a head," retorted Rollison.

"Don't!" Peter winced, sipped again, and then stiffened. "Great Scott, *you're* back!"

"You're improving," said Rollison.

"Well I'm damned!" exclaimed Peter. "I thought you'd run out on me." He finished his tea, put the cup down, and took on a shameface. "I've a vague memory of having said harsh things about you last night. Sorry. I was tight."

"Why?" asked Rollison.

Peter shrugged.

"It's as good a way as any of forgetting what a hellish racket I'm mixed up in," he said. He shivered. "Rolly, I'm not fooling. I'm scared. *How* I'm scared!"

"What else has happened?" asked Rollison mildly.

"Nothing much. I've been—followed. How I hate that feeling! I thought I'd finished with it when I got out of Germany, but it's as bad here. It's been happening for weeks. I wouldn't admit it at first, but I've got to now. Everywhere I go I'm watched. I'm *not* fooling, Rolly, it's true. Eyes follow me everywhere. Sometimes I think it's impossible for me to be alone. At the office, at home, in the streets, at a show, wherever I am and whatever I'm doing, eyes follow me."

"Not pink elephants?" murmured Rollison.

"Don't be an ass! I'm not blotto *all* the time." Peter ran his hands through his hair and went on in a hoarse voice: "I know it's crazy, but there it is. Whenever I look up people are watching me. They're not just glancing at me casually, it's a protracted stare. You—you know what it's like when you can feel that someone's looking at you from behind, and you turn round and they shift their gaze quickly? Well, it's like that."

"Who's chiefly responsible?" asked Rollison.

"That's one of the troubles. I can't *place* anyone. People at the office, in the departments, everywhere I go. As if I were a freak and they can't help staring at me." Peter put out a hand and watched his fingers trembling. "You see what it's doing to me? I was in a panic last night." He caught his breath. "I—I sometimes think I'm going mad!"

"I shouldn't worry about that," advised Rollison cheerfully. "These people are clever, you know, and want to unnerve you."

"But no one else seems to see them!"

Rollison chuckled.

"I saw one last night, and they're going to start seeing something more of me! Get up, and I'll tell you all about it."

Chapter Five

The Man Who Worked At Majors

Grice rubbed the big scar which ran from his cheek to his temple and crossed his legs. He was as good a listener as Peter, but his silence hinted at scepticism and created some disquiet. Rollison ignored the hint and dwelt at length on Peter's fears.

"I see," said Grice at last. "Some people would say that you ought to have reported last night."

"Would it have helped?" asked Rollison. "Your fellows were on the scene very quickly. The hunt was up before I left."

"And you wanted time to decide how much to tell me."

Rollison smiled. 'Unjust! You know all."

"I wish I could be sure," said Grice. He uncrossed his legs and smoothed down his brown coat. He was a dark man with a tanned, shiny face; his skin stretched so tight that the ridges on the bridge of his nose showed white. "Still, I suppose I'll have to take your word for it."

"Wise man," said Rollison. "What do you make of it?"

"I haven't had time to make anything of it yet. This man who might work at Majors—have you spoken to Lund about him?"

"He said the description might apply to any half-dozen men at Majors, and there's something in that. I'll recognise him again if he's there, but I doubt whether he will be."

"Rolly, what I want to know is—what are *you* going to do?"

"I don't know yet," declared Rollison. "There hasn't been much time. I'll consult you, of course."

"'Of course' nothing!" said Grice, and chuckled, "All right, I'll do all I can, and I'll welcome modest help from you. The first thing you might do is to go to Majors and try to find the man who fired at you. Where's the gun?"

Rollison went to the desk, opened a drawer and took out the gun which was still wrapped in a handkerchief. He handed it to Grice.

"I don't think you'll find any prints on Exhibit 'A'," he said; "our man wore gloves. Bright yellow on the road, dark cotton in the flat. Not a stranger to crime, Bill. Have you any reason to think there's trouble at Majors?"

"Only the usual city rumours when shares behave as they shouldn't," said Grice, "but it hasn't been brought to our notice officially. Have you met the great Romeo?"

"No, I've only seen him at a distance."

Grice laughed.

"I hope I'm present when you meet!" He stood up, slipping the gun into his pocket. "Lund's still here, you say?"

"Yes."

"I'll see him first and then go on to see the girl," decided Grice. "You can tell your young hopeful that he needn't haunt Ellerby Mews any longer, it's being watched. And seriously," went on Grice, "I'd like you to go to Majors. You might strike lucky."

"Fortune smiles on fools," quoth Rollison. "Peter Lund's given me permission to tell the whole story to Romeo, too!" He raised his voice: "Peter!"

Looking much more presentable, Peter came from his bedroom with remarkable promptness. Rollison introduced Grice, murmured pleasantries and platitudes and then left them together while he went to Majors.

Whatever the state of its shares on the market, Majors was busy. Peter's publicity brought the crowds. So, if the truth were told, did some of the commodities on sale. Romeo supervised all the buying for the store, and he had performed miracles. One could buy at

Majors goods which were not available elsewhere. There were queues in some of the departments. Harassed assistants dealt with equally harassed buyers, and tempers were short, Rollison heard comments from staff to clients which would not have been allowed elsewhere. He thought a great deal about that, for one of Peter's worries was incivility among the staff which no one appeared to be able to overcome.

A half-empty lift shot up after the gates had been slammed in his face.

"Not good," murmured Rollison.

A shopwalker came towards him, a tall but frail specimen with a hangdog look and scowl. He walked with his hands behind his back, Felix fashion, looking right and left but offering no help to the thronging crowds. His appearance was enough to intimidate seekers after information. He treated Rollison to a glare and went on his way.

"Not at all good," said Rollison to himself.

He changed his mind about the lift and walked about the ground floor. The only male assistants were in the men's department. Most of them were neatly dressed, all looked supercilious; none was the man of the road but several answered his description approximately. It was easy to understand Peter's comment.

Rollison went to the next floor.

Few men were on duty there, for it was exclusively for women. The fur *salon* had a quality and a spaciousness which was unlike the rest of Majors. Rollison's feet sank deep in the pile of a pale-blue carpet. There was a hush everywhere. He looked into each department, then went up to the third floor, where toys and books and games and gardening equipment jostled one another, and more men were on duty; his man was not.

The next floor was for miscellaneous goods. Romeo had recently introduced a theatre-ticket agency and *music*. Romeo talked italics. Here, too, was the restaurant, not yet crowded. Rollison made sure that his man was not about and went to the offices, on the fifth and top floor. Here quiet reigned until he went into the general office, which was a-hum and a-quiver with talk and typewriters and people on the move. It had the look of a prison compound at a time of excitement.

The private offices of the managers and directors led off a passage which could only be approached on this side by talking on one side of the general office. Rollison looked about him with even greater care, but his man was not there. He did not seriously think the fellow would be; disappearance was wise after the failure of the night before.

A fussy little tight-lipped woman approached him.

"Excuse me, customers aren't allowed up here." She was offensive in her firmness.

"Not even with complaints?" asked Rollison.

"Complaints should be made to the supervisor of the floor concerned," she snapped. "Customers are not allowed here."

"Where does one see Mr. Romeo?" asked Rollison.

She was not beaten even by the magic name.

"Have you an appointment?"

"I have a letter from Mr. Peter Lund."

"All right, give it to me," said the woman, "and I will find out if he can see you." She looked at him suspiciously. "If you want to see the staff manager, he's three doors along."

"I want to see Mr. Romeo," insisted Rollison, and produced a note which Peter had hastily scribbled for him. The woman took it and read it, then turned, threw "Wait here," over her shoulder and trotted off. Rollison looked at her departing back without favour. Hers was typical of the service now in existence at Majors. Was Romeo blind to it?

Rollison did not wait, but followed her.

She tapped on a door on which was painted in gilt letters, *Augustus Romeo, Managing Director*, then opened it. The door closed silently behind her. The tap-tap-tap of typewriters came as if from a long way off. Rollison strolled along the passage, and located Peter's office with, *Peter Lund, Publicity Director*, on the door, also in gilt lettering. The next door to it, that of a corner room, was labelled, *R. Calvert, Staff Manager.* Romeo's door opened, and voices sounded in the passage. "Right-ho," a man said, "I'll look after that."

"Of course you will, Calvert, and *at once*." That booming voice was Romeo's, and Rollison, who had heard it several times in night-clubs and in other places of entertainment, recognised it on the first word. "It isn't good enough, not good enough by a long way," declared Romeo; "you *must* get a new spirit among the staff, it is essential. *Service* is the motto, supplies and service! You can get what you want at Majors. Ah, that's a good one. What do you think, Calvert?"

"Very good indeed," said Calvert.

At first his voice had been drowned by Romeo's. Now it came clearly, making Rollison stiffen and stare towards the door. The little woman came out and, without a glance towards him, walked back towards the spot where she had left him. Calvert, the staff manager, backed into the passage, still speaking.

He was the man of the road.

Chapter Six

Calvert Makes Haste

"Calvert! Just a moment!" Romeo bellowed the words as the staff manager was about to turn. Rollison caught a glimpse of his profile; voice and face were the same. Calvert stood in the doorway with his hand on the handle, and Romeo went on: "There mustn't be *any* mistake this time. Your selection of men for shopwalking has been deplorable—deplorable. They are sour of visage, harsh of voice and impolite of manner. You *must* do better."

"I'll do all I can," promised Calvert.

"See that you do. Now off with you!"

Undoubtedly Calvert would have liked to place the toe of his shoe in a soft part of Romeo's anatomy. He was flushed as he turned round and walked towards Rollison. So angry was he that although he saw Rollison he did not immediately recognise him. Rollison stared with obvious interest and suddenly Calvert stopped in his tracks. The blood drained from his cheeks, his eyes widened and he drew in a sharp breath.

"Good morning," said Rollison politely.

Romeo's door closed softly.

Calvert gaped. Rollison made as if to pass, showing no sign of recognition; he did not want Calvert to panic. He actually touched the handle of Romeo's door when Calvert gripped his shoulder and spun him round; they were only a yard apart. Calvert's breath coming in quick, sharp gasps, he searched Rollison's face as if praying that he was mistaken.

"Yes?" asked Rollison mildly.

"You—" sighed Calvert.

Then he kicked Rollison on the shin.

Even without the bruises the kick would have hurt, and Rollison staggered back against the wall. Calvert thrust out a hand to try to push him down, then turned and raced along the passage. Romeo's door opened, and his mammoth figure was outlined in the doorway.

"Good gracious me!" exclaimed Romeo.

Rollison snapped: "Telephone downstairs, tell them to stop Calvert from leaving. Police!" he added, and sped in the staff manager's wake. The pain slowed him down, but that wore off. He heard a door slam; he reached the general office. Calvert was half-way across it, rushing towards the far door. Clerks and typists stared at him in wide-eyed astonishment. He looked over his shoulder and saw Rollison. On the instant, he grabbed a tin filing-tray from a desk and flung it over his shoulder. Papers flew in all directions; a girl gasped, the tray clattered to the floor and Rollison jumped over it.

Calvert reached the door,

"Stop him!" cried Rollison.

"*Stop him!*" bellowed Romeo.

Had Rollison looked behind him he would have seen a sight indeed. Romeo was too fat to pass with comfort between the rows of desks. He was too fat to run. But he was moving with a shambling gait, swaying this way and that in order to squeeze past the desks, waving a clenched fist wildly. Where he found the breath to shout "*Stop him, stop him!*" was a mystery. The staff stood up as one man and gaped, and an office boy near the far door jumped forward, pulled the door open and rushed after Calvert a yard or two in front of Rollison. Calvert was standing by the lift gates. The lift was moving slowly to a standstill. The boy, eyes bright with determination and fists clenched, rushed forward.

Calvert kicked him.

The kick caught the lad on the side of the face. Rollison heard the sharp crack, and anger against Calvert welled up inside him. The kick lifted the boy off the floor, and then he dropped like a stone. Calvert pulled at the lift gates, but they jammed. He turned right, towards the stairs. Rollison had to step carefully over the boy. Calvert dodged him by inches and clattered down the stairs, which were uncarpeted just there.

"*Stop him!*" squealed Romeo.

The boy was unconscious. A girl rushed out and dropped on her knees beside him, crying in alarm.

Rollison started down the stairs. Calvert had lost much of his advantage but was half-way down, near a bend in the stairs. He turned his head once, saw Rollison, and promptly jumped a whole flight. Rollison skimmed down them, not daring to take the jump because of his bruised legs. A man coming up the stairs shouted, and went down under a blow from Calvert's wide-flung arms. Two or three other people were on the stairs. Calvert pushed them aside. One slipped; they all slipped. Calvert passed them and Rollison followed him, jumping over outstretched arms. A woman and her child were on the next landing, and the woman snatched the child up.

Calvert headed for the next flight of stairs, with Rollison half a flight behind him.

A solid phalanx of people was coming up the staircase below. No one could hope to brush them aside or push past them. Calvert spun round on one foot and rushed into the department. He knocked a woman over, then raced across the carpeted floor, his footsteps making a heavy thudding noise. Assistants and customers gaped, those in the way dodged quickly to one side. Rollison made more speed on the level ground, and the path was cleared for him as if by magic. Toys being displayed for a customer were spread out on the floor in front of Calvert. Calvert put a hand on a counter and sprang over it, then rushed towards a door in the far corner. He crashed into a bookcase and sent it flying, sent books tumbling from the shelves. Halfway across the floor he grabbed a solid toy engine from a shelf, turned and flung it at Rollison.

It crashed into a glass case.

Nearer the corner, Calvert dragged a cash register from a counter, turned, and heaved it towards Rollison, who was only four yards behind him, Rollison dodged and the register crashed with a noise like an explosion and a great ringing of bells. Money fell out and rolled in all directions. Rollison made his way past it, and was still only four yards behind when Calvert reached a door, the top panel of which was glass.

Through the glass he saw the man rush towards a secondary flight of stairs, but he did not see him *on* the stairs.

He paused.

Chaos approaching panic spread behind him, but he stood quite still watching the door. There was no sign of Calvert, hut he was sure that the man was hiding behind it, ready to push it into his face if he went through. He stepped forward slowly, then ducked. Screams and cries were corning from behind him, and above the babel of sound a woman's voice could be heard saying: *"Really, really, really!"*

Calvert's head appeared at the glass panel; and then his hand at the side of the door. He held a gun.

"Get away!" cried Rollison to people near him. "Get away!" He picked up a heavy book-end from a counter and flung it at Calvert's hand. It struck the door and the hand was snatched away. Rollison rushed through. The door had knocked Calvert against the wall, and he had lost his grip on the gun. Rollison swung round and closed with him, grabbing at his wrist. Calvert brought his knee up, but missed Rollison's groin. Immediately behind him was a railing, protecting the narrow staircase. Rollison forced him over it, feeling the man's hot breath on his cheeks. Calvert was writhing and gasping and kicking, but Rollison had his throat in one hand and his right wrist in the other. The man bent backwards. He went farther – so far that Rollison was afraid his back would break.

He saw the glaring eyes …

Then something hit him on the back of the head.

It was a sharp blow, not enough to put him out but enough to make him lose his grip. He did not see who struck him. He relaxed, and Calvert straightened up, pushed him back, and then went towards the stairs. From the door came a new falsetto voice: "*Stop him!*"

That was Romeo.

Calvert reached the top of the stairs, slipped, and slid down. Rollison was holding his head and swaying to and fro. The landing was suddenly crowded with people; it was impossible to tell who had hit him. He tried to go forward but Romeo got in front of him and was wedged between two men and the railings. The tight-lipped woman was near him.

Rollison peered over the edge, Calvert had reached the landing below and, with his astonishing agility, vaulted over the railings and landed safely. Romeo was still squealing, and a string of men and youths was rushing down the stairs, but Rollison did not think that they would catch the man.

Rollison stood in a corner of the wrecked department with a telephone in his hand. Romeo towered over him like a protecting Colossus, breathing helpful platitudes. At the other end of the line Grice was saying: "You're quite sure, Rolly?"

"Yes, there's no argument. Calvert—"

"C-A-L-V-E-R-T," breathed Romeo.

"Who works at Majors, and his private address is—"

"Seventeen, Mayhew Street, Hendon," hissed Romeo.

"Seventeen, Mayhew Street, Hendon."

"All right, thanks," said Grice. "You sound a bit winded."

"I'm surprised that I've got any breath left at all," said Rollison, "Don't lose him."

"I'll see to it," promised Grice.

When Romeo and Rollison reached the top floor the general office was in a state of commotion which subsided miraculously when Romeo opened the door. Girls and men who had been standing and talking excitedly returned to their seats, and in most cases put up a creditable show of being at work. Only the tight-lipped woman who had greeted Rollison when he had first arrived kept standing. She advanced purposefully towards Roliisen and Romeo.

"Put them to work," ordered Romeo. "Too much time has been lost already. I will speak to them later, when I have a fuller knowledge of what lies behind this affair. Come along, my friend."

Rollison thought that Romeo did not much like the tight-lipped woman. Nor did she appear to like Romeo, while she bent a look of acute disapproval on Rollison, who smiled brightly and followed the fat man.

They reached the private office passage.

A clean-limbed, fair-haired youngster was standing in the doorway of Romeo's office. From inside there came a babble of voices. The young man hurried forward.

"Everyone is greatly worried, Mr. Romeo, in case—"

"There is no need for anyone to be worried," declared Romeo. "I do not want to be disturbed for half an hour. See that the toy department is being properly cleared and made ready for reopening early this afternoon. Or rather, *before* lunch—not that they will get it done much before two," he added with a quick, unexpected smile. He strode past the young man and entered his office. Several middle-aged and well-dressed men were gathered there, and they turned and looked at Romeo as at an oracle.

Romeo surveyed them for an appreciable time. Then: "There is no cause for alarm, gentlemen. I shall be able to make a statement later in the morning."

One of the men exclaimed: "So you know!"

"Know what?" asked Romeo, and added testily, "I know that Calvert appears to have disgraced himself."

"But he's got away with *thousands*!" exclaimed the other. "Did you know *that*?"

Chapter Seven

Rollison And Romeo

Romeo was obviously taken completely by surprise, but Rollison admired the fat man's perfect self-control. He blinked once or twice and then waved a hand; a diamond ring sparkled in the sunlight which shone through the window.

"Has he, indeed! Well, we know how to deal with absconding rascals. The police are already searching for him. You will forgive me, gentlemen, but I have a private matter to discuss with my friend here." He patted Rollison's shoulder.

Rollison smiled apologetically.

"Could we be told more about the theft?" he asked.

That was the signal for which the men had been waiting; all of them began to talk at once, until Romeo let out a bellow and they stopped. Only the young man who had first spoken went on. He explained quickly and with admirable precision. This, as Mr. Romeo knew, was pay day – the last day of the month. The wages had been brought from the bank and taken to the cashier's office. A few minutes before the sensation Calvert had gone there and said that Mr. Romeo wanted the money; Calvert had taken it to his own office. The speaker, who, it transpired, was Romeo's secretary, knew nothing about such a request.

"And there was none," declared Romeo.

"That's what we mean," said another man. "He's got away with it!" He did not take the news as calmly as Romeo.

"How many bags were there?" asked Rollison.

"Three."

"All fairly heavy?"

"The copper and silver bags were *very* heavy."

"Then he didn't take the cash with him," remarked Rollison. Romeo nipped the end of his nose between his thumb and forefinger and gave a tight-lipped, mirthless smile.

"Obviously he did not. He was in great alarm. You might look for the bags, Hilary. If they are not found, draw another cheque and I will sign it immediately. Now, gentlemen, *if* you please."

They filed out.

Hilary closed the door and Romeo exuded a long, slow breath and went to his desk. It was a fine desk of carved mahogany, with a leather top. Only two telephones, a blotting-pad and a silver inkstand stood upon it. He rounded the desk, bent down and took out a bottle and some glasses from a cupboard.

"It is a little early," he said apologetically, "but I feel the need of a stimulant. I hope you'll join me."

"Not now, thanks," said Rollison.

Rollison watched him pour himself out a stiff peg, then add a splash of soda and drink deeply. "Ah!" He sat down and waved to a chair; his own huge chair was only just large enough for him. He took out a box of cigarettes and pushed them across the desk. "Do smoke. You are a remarkable man, Mr. Rollison." Romeo waved a hand.

"I suppose you often feel, as I do, the appalling weariness which comes over one when dealing with *ordinary* men. What is it they lack, Rollison? Some spark, some glow of intelligence, some—perhaps I am a little harsh. Perhaps I am one of the fortunate few whose mind, being above the average, finds it easy to become impatient, even angry, with others. I was with my fellow-directors just now. Do you know, the *only* man on my board with whom I never feel irritated is young Peter Lund. Now there is an intelligent fellow! He gave you a note of introduction, didn't he? Yes, that is right. Even before I had seen you I knew that a man introduced by Peter Lund would not be an ordinary man! And of course"—a faint smile shone in his large brown eyes—"I had heard of you. Who hasn't, indeed?"

"I'm not so notorious as that," protested Rollison.

Romeo gave a deep, rich chuckle.

"I'm not so sure! There is one sign of distinction which is a never-failing guide to character, you know—a soubriquet, a nickname, dubbed upon one by others. Yours I know—the Toff. I am *very* glad to meet you."

"I wouldn't have missed this either," said Rollison. He sat down and took a cigarette. "Curiosity isn't your leading suit, is it?"

Romeo pursed his lips.

"It depends what you mean by curiosity. I am extremely anxious to know what caused that astonishing incident. Now, Mr. Rollison, shall we begin at the beginning? Why did Peter ask such an eminent man to come to see me?"

Rollison hesitated, and then said mildly: "He's frightened out of his wits and would like me to help him."

"As bad as that?" murmured Romeo. "I knew that he was not happy, of course; that he had some cause for alarm. I'm distressed that he is really frightened. May I ask what it is about—and so show my curiosity?"

"He suspects funny business inside Majors," said Rollison. "He doesn't know what, and he couldn't confide in you or the police, but he's not happy about the way things are going. Nor are you, I fancy. Shares falling, service atrocious, the general atmosphere of the store offsetting the good that brilliant publicity is doing—it *is* odd, isn't it?"

"Odd," murmured Romeo, watching him intently.

"Yes. Peter was so worried that he came to see me some weeks ago. We're old friends. He talked in confidence, wanting to know if I could make anything of it. The first noticeable result was that, from the time he came to see me, other, unknown people showed a great interest in him," added Rollison. "He is followed everywhere he goes, and I think he's been threatened once or twice—directly or indirectly."

"I wish he had told me," said Romeo, sounding peeved.

"He's asked me to tell you," said Rollison. He leaned forward, and added impressively: "It isn't imagination. Last night—"

He told the man where he had first met Calvert.

Romeo sat very still until the narrative was finished, when he picked up his glass and finished the drink. Then he drew heavily on his cigarette.

"I see. Calvert recognised you here, became alarmed, and fled. I do not see how that can be reconciled with the theft of the wages," said Romeo. He leaned down and clicked a switch hidden from Rollison by the desk. Then he spoke as if to someone by his side. "Hilary, have those bags been found yet?"

He looked towards a small window built in the wall between his office and Hilary's.

A disembodied voice, just recognisable as Hilary's, floated into the room.

"No, sir. They were last seen by a typist in Mr. Calvert's office."

"Have you sent for the police?"

"I'm waiting for instructions, sir."

"Have you told the store detectives?"

"Yes, sir, and they are making inquiries."

"That will do for the present," said Romeo, and clicked the talking-box silent. "How do you account for it, Rollison? You met Calvert by accident, as it were; he could not have known that you would be here, and so his flight at that moment and in that manner was presumably unpremeditated. He certainly did not have time to make up that absurd story about bringing the money to me, dispose of it, and then make off."

"No," agreed Rollison.

"Then how *do* you account for it?"

"My guess is that he knew that he had been seen last night, knew that he might be traced to Majors, planned the flight with the money and lost his nerve when he came face to face with me," Rollison said.

"Then who took the money away?"

"An accomplice."

"Inside Majors?"

"Probably," said Rollison.

"Yes. Yes, I think I have to agree with you there," Romeo conceded, "But surely someone saw the bags being removed from this floor. The lift-girls are not *all* blind. You know, Rollison, in some way this is a relief, a great relief. I have been worried by the kind of employee we have been getting lately. A most unsatisfactory type—I had occasion to complain to Calvert about it this morning, doubtless you heard me. There has been widespread dissatisfaction among the staff, too, although we pay them well—really well, I assure you. I have put it down to one or two unpleasant elements, agitators by nature and perhaps by training, here to spread dissatisfaction. These are not days when one can pick and choose one's staff, and I assumed that Calvert, who was not a fool, selected the best he could. *Now* I wonder whether Calvert was deliberately employing men and women whom he knew would be unsatisfactory. What do you think of that?"

"It could be," murmured Rollison.

"I think it is almost certainly the case," declared Romeo. "Peter thought that someone *here* was responsible. This appears to prove him right. Perhaps we shall have no more trouble now that Calvert has gone."

"I shouldn't be too optimistic," advised Rollison.

"No, no! I shall take every conceivable precaution, but forewarned, as they say, is forearmed! I do wish Peter had shown sufficient confidence in me to tell me about his anxieties." Romeo leaned forward and went on impressively: "Mr. Rollison, do not misunderstand me. But certain expenses are involved in a matter of this kind, and I assure you that I am as anxious as Peter is to find out the *whole* truth. We have agreed that someone inside Majors is probably an accomplice of Calvert's, and although I have a great admiration for the police I think that in some respects you might be able to do better than they. Will you try? And, of course, allow me to pay you—ah—handsome expenses."

"Make out a cheque to St. Oswald's Hospital," said Rollison promptly.

"How generous of you!"

"Generous of *you*," echoed Rollison, who was keeping deliberately subdued. Romeo fascinated him. There were few men with the same aplomb. He liked Romeo; whether he could trust him was a different matter.

"The police will want to know everything, of course," he said.

"Of course!"

"There's nothing you want to keep back?"

"My dear Rollison, that isn't worthy of you," protested Romeo. "Why should I require to keep anything back?"

"No conditions and no restrictions?" asked Rollison.

"None whatsoever!"

"It's a deal," decided Rollison. "You know more about the campaign against Majors than you've told me yet, don't you?"

Romeo put his head on one side but did not immediately answer. As if from a long way off voices, the sound of typewriters and the sound of telephone bells ringing came to Rollison's ears. Footsteps passed in the passage every few minutes; voices outside were muted, as if it were forbidden to talk loudly within earshot of the great Romeo.

Rollison continued to study the man closely.

Romeo was dressed immaculately in dark brown. He had a red rose in his buttonhole. His brown hair shone, and was brushed flat on a rounded cranium. He had a high-bridged nose, but his features were large and his nose was not too big in proportion. His lips were full, the underlip thrust forward a little. His eyes were good. He created an impression of great intelligence, and was well groomed to his finger-tips.

This was the man who had returned from the United States with the avowed intention of performing miracles with Majors, who had partly succeeded, but was apparently finding his efforts nullified by someone unknown to Rollison but perhaps not to Romeo. This was the man about whom rumour had spread fast, whose antics on the Stock Exchange had troubled many people but who had never gone too far. If Grice were to be believed, he had sailed close to the wind in America but had always stopped in time.

Rollison wished that he knew more about him.

The silence lasted for a considerable time, and then Romeo straightened up and murmured: "What makes you suggest that I know more?"

"Because you're not a fool," said Rollison. "You wouldn't sit back and see your shares falling without wanting to know why, and you wouldn't be so calm about it if you didn't think you could stop the fall. You certainly can't stop it if you don't know what's causing it, therefore you have a shrewd idea of the motive."

"I *see*," breathed Romeo, his eyes glowing with approval. "I thought you were a man of exceptional intelligence, now I know! I congratulate you on your reasoning—and of course it is sound, you are quite right. I believe that I know who is trying to ruin *me*, through Majors. Mr. Rollison, I am a successful man."

He said that as if uttering a challenge, and Rollison agreed promptly.

"Successful men make enemies!" declared Romeo.

"Some of them do," corrected Rollison.

"Oh, nonsense, *all* of them do. I will tell you the name of the man who, I feel sure, is trying to avenge himself for an early failure which he attributes to me. Now he is powerful, as I am powerful, and one would have thought that he would be satisfied to rest on his laurels. But no! Nothing will satisfy him, except—"

Romeo stopped abruptly.

He had been looking into Rollison's eyes, but his gaze shifted towards the door. Someone had been walking along the passage but had stopped. Rollison glanced quickly over his shoulder and saw that the door was opening. He jumped to his feet. Romeo stood up and moved swiftly to one side, while Rollison crossed to the door, which was still opening very slowly and without a sound.

Chapter Eight

More Cause For Alarm

Romeo moved with cat-like tread until he stood against the wall behind the door. Rollison reached the door and stood just behind it. He thought he heard someone breathing. He watched a spot near the handle, expecting to see a gun thrust into the room, but all that happened was that the door continued to open slowly and without a sound. The clatter of typewriters came more clearly, and someone's voice was raised on a telephone.

Voices sounded nearer at hand.

"If Mr. Romeo says—" began young Hilary.

On the instant, the door stopped opening. Rollison snatched at the inside handle, but it was pulled out of his grasp. The door slammed. They heard Hilary exclaim in alarm, then the sound of people running along the passage. There followed a thud, as if someone had fallen, and after that further footsteps, which faded rapidly.

Rollison pulled open the door and strode out into the passage. Hilary and a man with a tuft of golden hair were on the floor near the counter. Hilary was scrambling to his feet and he turned and gave chase to whoever had felled him. Rollison went after him.

They heard the whine of the lift, and Hilary pulled up short.

"We've lost the beggar," he growled.

"Who was it?"

"I don't know. He was peering round Romeo's door—Mr. Romeo's door," corrected Hilary hastily, for Romeo appeared in the passage. "I didn't like the look of him and he didn't like the look of us."

"Did he have a weapon?"

"I didn't see one," said Hilary. "I hope you're all right, sir," he added, as Romeo came up.

Romeo waved a hand.

"I am always all right when I am with Mr. Rollison," he declared. "The rascal has gone, I suppose," The lift had since stopped. "Did you see him clearly, Hilary? Williams?"

"*I* saw him vividly!" exclaimed Williams, who was rubbing his cheek gingerly. "He was a small, dark-clad man, a most unpleasant-looking fellow. Are—*are* you all right, sir?"

"I am. What are you doing here, instead of in the department, Williams? Really, you are most trying! You need to be there to superintend the tidying, not wandering about up here. Please go downstairs and look after it. What do you want, Hilary?"

"I've brought the wages cheque, sir,"

"So the bags have not been found." Romeo turned into the office, took the cheque from Hilary's hand, signed it with a flourish and then handed it back, A crestfallen Williams had already gone. "Was that description of the man accurate?" he asked Hilary.

"It wasn't far wrong," agreed Hilary.

"Had you ever seen him before?"

"No, sir."

"I hope we shall see him again," said Romeo. "Tell the store detectives to make *quite* sure that unauthorised persons are not allowed to come to this floor. Let them employ agency men if there are not enough on the staff. We can't have strangers wandering about the offices like that, we have already lost a small fortune through such carelessness."

"I'll tell them," promised Hilary patiently.

He nodded and went out.

Romeo picked up another cigarette, and said slowly: "That would appear to give me more cause for alarm, Mr. Rollison, You assumed, as I did, that the marauder came with evil intent. I *quite* expected to be fired at. It really is most trying!" he added peevishly, as if he did not realise the quality of that understatement. "It must stop. What was I saying to you before we were interrupted?"

"You were going to name your arch enemy," said Rollison.

"Oh yes. I—con*found* the telephone!"

He broke off, turned swiftly, and snatched at the receiver. *"Hallo!"* he boomed, in a voice which must have carried to the general office. *"Yes! … Who?"*

In front of Rollison's eyes, he wilted.

He was standing at the desk, one hand pressing against it, the sun shining on his polished nails and the diamond ring. He made a majestic figure, and at first there was a touch of irritation in his voice which matched his mood. Then he changed, and seemed to sag. He tried to sit on the table as he listened, stood upright again and, still holding the telephone and paying attention to what was being said, he moved round the desk and dropped into the capacious chair. He did not look at Rollison and appeared to be unaware that anyone else was in the office.

Whoever was speaking to him took a long time.

"I—see," he said at last. "Yes, yes, I will look after it. Of course not … I have given you my word," he went on, with a slight return of his bombastic manner. "I shall not break it. Good-bye."

He replaced the receiver and then turned to face Rollison.

"I am—grieved," declared Romeo. He had lost colour, and there was a scared look in his eyes, not unlike the look in Peter Lund's. He pulled open a drawer and took out a cheque-book while Rollison watched him with quickening interest. He drew a cheque, tore it out and pushed it across the desk. "That is what I undertook to do for the hospital," he said. "I am sorry that I cannot give you the commission which I had in mind, Events—events have changed."

"Rather quickly," said Rollison sharply.

"No one regrets it more than I. I am sorry. It is not for myself. I cannot continue to see you, Rollison, I must ask you not to come here again. The matter will be handled by the police, to whom I cannot deny admittance." He rose, picked up the cheque and thrust it into Rollison's hand. "I want you to accept my assurance that I can do *nothing* else, Rollison. It—it greatly grieves me. I have had a severe shock," He was perspiring freely, and sat down again, taking out a white silk handkerchief. It billowed about his face. Just for a second Rollison saw the gleam in his eyes, as if Romeo were desperately anxious that he should take him seriously and was watching to make sure of his reaction.

Rollison put the cheque in his pocket without looking at it.

"You know, you're not being wise," he said. "Fear's a bad thing and someone's frightened you."

"Please do not make difficulties now," begged Romeo.

Rollison said, "I'm worried about Peter, you know."

"Yes, yes. We all are, we all are."

"And I shouldn't take marching orders even from him," said Rollison. Romeo stared up at him, limp and miserable. Rollison strengthened his voice. "This won't do, Romeo! If a man can scare the wits out of you with five minutes on the telephone, it's time—"

"Stop!" cried Romeo. He jumped up, his hand upraised. "I tell you there is nothing more you can do for me now. You must go. I know my own business. I know what risks I am prepared to run, and risking *her* is not one of them!"

"Her!" echoed Rollison.

"My wife," snapped Romeo. "I will face danger, I will not let her face it. Rollison, I do not wish to have to send for assistance, it would be undignified and ungrateful for me to have you *thrown* out, but I—"

He stopped again, just as he had done when the door had opened before, and stared over Rollison's shoulder. Rollison swung round. There had been no sound of footsteps, but the door was thrust open
…

A woman entered.

She was a lovely, smiling creature, wearing a dark red suit with a wide-brimmed hat. She was not young but unquestionably she was beautiful. She walked gracefully across the office, smiling at Romeo, sparing only a casual glance for Rollison.

"Hallo, darling!" she greeted.

"Why—why, Chloe!" gasped Romeo.

"I didn't think I'd get back today," said the woman gaily. "I managed to get a seat on the morning plane, and—"

"Plane!" echoed Romeo. "You—you shouldn't fly, my dear; you know I think it's dangerous. Really, you—Oh, I'd forgotten. You don't know Mr. Rollison. My wife, Mr. Rollison."

Chloe Romeo smiled radiantly at Rollison.

"How are you?"

"How are you?" said Rollison at the same moment.

There was a long pause.

"We—we have had a little trouble here, my dear," said Romeo awkwardly. "That rascal Calvert has absconded." He was looking at Rollison, not his wife, and there was a plea in his eyes – he wanted Rollison to leave at once. "Mr, Rollison nearly stopped him; we are most grateful. I—" He stopped short.

Rollison looked at Chloe.

Just for a moment, when Calvert's name had been mentioned, there had been a gleam in her eyes, one that might have been of surprise or alarm. It was gone in a flash, but it warned Rollison that Calvert meant something to the woman.

He did not hesitate longer but held out his hand.

"Good-bye," he said.

"Thank you so much," said Mrs. Romeo.

"A thousand thanks, a thousand!" exclaimed Romeo. He rushed round the table, took Rollison's arm and propelled him towards the door. "Thank you, thank you. *Thank you*," he whispered as they reached the door. He opened it and thrust Rollison into the passage. Rollison's last glimpse of the office was of Romeo's wife standing quite still, like a lovely dummy, and Romeo's eyes showing great relief.

The door closed.

Rollison turned towards Hilary's office, thrust the door open and stepped inside. No one was there. A big flat-topped desk was loaded with telephones and with another speaking-box. The walls were lined with files, except the one adjoining Romeo's room. The little window in this was closed. Rollison crossed to it and opened it a fraction. He could not see into the room beyond but he could hear.

He heard a kiss!

"Oh, Gus!" exclaimed Chloe Romeo. "Mind my lipstick!"

"I—I'm sorry, my dear," murmured Romeo. "I am so glad to see you back safe and sound. I hate it when you go away, you know, you go away too often. I—I *need* you, my dear, I'm never happy when I'm on my own."

"Silly!" chided Chloe.

Rollison raised his eyebrows at that.

"We've had just a little trouble," said Romeo, repeating himself and proving to Rollison that he was really upset. "It isn't much, but it's distressing. Calvert's villainy shocked me. You've never liked that man, have you?"

"Never," declared Chloe roundly.

'I wonder,' murmured Rollison to himself.

"Now sit down and make yourself comfortable," urged Romeo, "and we'll have some lunch at Larry's. Would you like that?"

"I'd love it!"

"Good," enthused Romeo. "Good. How is your mother? And everyone in Dublin?"

"They're fine," said Chloe. "Everyone was very glad to see me, of course, and they hope you'll be able to come over next time. It *was* sweet of you to send me those flowers, Gus."

"Flowers?" ejaculated Romeo.

"Yes. The lovely roses," said Chloe.

"I—ah, yes, yes, of course," said Romeo. He seemed to have gone completely to pieces since his wife had arrived, and if this were any criterion of their usual conversation he did not make the demand of intelligence on his wife that he made on others. He seemed a different man, weaker, spineless. "Now do sit down, my dear, and have a cigarette—would you care for a drink?"

"Not yet," refused Chloe. Her words were light, her manner automatic; she seemed to Rollison like an animated doll.

"You're wise—very wise," said Romeo. "I won't be long—not a minute longer than I can help. I just want a word with Hilary."

He wanted more than that; he did not want his wife to hear what he said or he would have used the talking-box. As it was, his words made Rollison turn from the little window and look about the office for a hiding-place. There was one large steel cupboard which might hold him. He opened it, and it clanged; there was room inside. He stepped in, pulling the door and leaving it open only an inch or two.

The office door opened.

"Hilary!" Romeo stopped. "Confound the man!" Rollison thought that he was standing in the doorway and surveying the apparently empty office. "Where is he? I—Oh, Hilary!"

Footsteps sounded in the passage.

"Why aren't you here when I want you?" asked Romeo, testily. He closed the door and lowered his voice so that there was no chance of it being heard in the next room. "Hilary , did I tell you to arrange for some roses to be sent to Mrs. Romeo in Dublin?"

"Why, no," answered Hilary, startled.

"Did you send any?"

"No, not without instructions."

"Someone did, in my name. It's puzzling." Romeo was at the half-way stage between his normal self and the broken man who had taken orders over the telephone because, it seemed, his wife had been threatened. "Well, forget about it. Now listen to me, Hilary. You are not to allow anyone to alarm my wife. I don't want her to know what happened downstairs—do you understand?"

"Yes, sir," said Hilary. "Is she back?"

"Yes, in my office. I am going downstairs and I don't want anyone to go in there."

"I'll put Jordon on the door, sir."

"Yes, do that." Romeo walked heavily across the office and went out. Hilary picked up the telephone; Rollison heard the clear ting of the bell. Hilary gave instructions to the man Jordon, presumably a store detective, then replaced the receiver. There was a click, as of a lighter being used, followed by a smell of Virginian tobacco smoke.

"That—ruddy—woman!" exclaimed Hilary, in a deep voice.

Rollison pushed the door open.

"She looks quite a picture," he remarked pleasantly.

Hilary jumped up from his chair. His eyes were ablaze and he doubled his fists and held them in front of him, as if expecting an attack. Only when he recognised Rollison did he relax. Hostility quickly replaced the alarm in his eyes. In his surprise he had dropped the cigarette, which smouldered on the carpet; there was a faint smell of burning.

"You'd better not set the place on fire," advised Rollison.

Hilary glared, then bent down and picked up the cigarette. He tossed it into an ash-tray without putting it out, glancing away from Rollison only for a moment. The silence lengthened. Rollison wanted to make Hilary break it, and the man clenched his fists again and stepped forward.

"What are you doing here?"

"Some people call it detecting," said Rollison airily. He took out his cigarette-case and proffered it. Hilary made as if to wave it away, then changed his mind and took one. Rollison flicked his lighter. Hilary did not say 'Thanks', but drew deeply on the cigarette. "Don't you like the lovely lady?"

"That's no business of yours."

"Then I'll draw my own conclusions," said Rollison. He leaned on a chair and smiled into the youngster's face. "I'm not a ghost, you know, and I was snooping because I wanted to hear how Romeo treated his wife."

"I could tell you that," said Hilary bitterly. "He treats her as if she were made of gold. Like a goddess! I can't understand how he can make—" He broke off abruptly.

"Such a fool of himself," completed Rollison.

Hilary shrugged, then burst out: 'She hasn't an idea in the whole of her head. She's—she's nothing but a pretty doll, and a man like Romeo has to throw himself away on her. All she married him for was his money. And he was snared by her looks, which—But damn it!" exploded Hilary. "I shouldn't be talking to you like this. What *are* you doing here? What right have you to be in my office while I'm out?"

"None," said Rollison handsomely. "I apologise. Romeo asked me to leave, hut I wanted to find out what he said to his wife. And I was interested in the roses which he didn't send to her. For the rest—How well do you know Peter Lund?"

Hilary's eyes brightened.

"Pretty well."

"You know he's in some bother?"

"I fancied so, but he doesn't talk about it," said Hilary. "He can be pretty close, you know. I thought he drank too much once or twice, too, but—" He shrugged his shoulders. "What has Peter got to do with it?"

"I'm working at his invitation."

"Oh!" said Hilary. "Here?"

"Partly. He has a fixed idea that there's some trouble at Majors—"

"And there was! Calvert's been picking the worst possible men for shopwalking and supervising. He ought to have been kicked out weeks ago. I—But I'm still talking too much," Hilary added, giving a one-sided grin. "Calvert was the trouble all right and you obviously took a hand in getting rid of him. Thanks."

"A pleasure," murmured Rollison. "But he wasn't alone."

"I don't follow you."

"Someone made off with the money-bags. Someone else was poking about in Romeo's room half an hour ago. But we can't talk here," said Rollison. "Shall we have lunch together?"

"I'm booked," said Hilary. "I can't avoid it." He seemed really sorry.

"Then dinner tonight," suggested Rollison. "I'll be at Ligaro's in Hinden Street at half past seven. I shall probably bring Peter along, and he'll vouch for me," he added amiably.

"I shouldn't tell Romeo that I was about, if I were you, and I shouldn't tell Romeo what you think of his wife!"

"I won't." Hilary grinned shamefacedly.

"Then I won't, either," Rollison assured him. "You might concentrate on thinking about any odd business you've had here in the last few months, especially about Calvert, and whether Calvert's had any strange visitors. Because," added Rollison with forced lightness, "I think Romeo is in for a packet of trouble unless some of us rally round."

Hilary brushed his hair back from his forehead.

"There is *something* wrong," he admitted. "I— But I'll see you tonight."

"That's fine," said Rollison, and went out.

He thought that Hilary had taken everything more calmly than he should; it was as if the youngster had wanted to put up a show of defiance but actually intended to talk freely—almost too freely. It was not normal that a secretary should express himself so strongly about his employer's wife.

There was nothing really normal about Majors.

Chapter Nine

A Job For Jolly

Rollison leaned back in the chair at his desk and regarded Jolly with some attention. If Jolly were puzzled he did not say so; nor did he look it. Snub Higginbottom was standing by the trophy wall, with a one-sided grin on his face. Rollison had been in for twenty minutes and had been busy with correspondence but was now at ease.

"Is there anything more, sir?" asked Jolly.

"Yes," said Rollison, and asked deliberately, "How would you like to apply for a job?"

Snub's smile faded, for Rollison looked serious.

"With no great enjoyment, sir, I assure you," answered Jolly. "It would largely depend on the circumstances, if I may say so."

"You're exactly the man," declared Rollison. "I had a careful look at half a dozen of them, and you would beat them into a cocked hat. They're short of them, too, I believe. You have just the manner, the training, the courtesy—if I may say so."

"Thank you, sir."

"And the experience would come," said Rollison. He grinned. "But I'm not playing fair! I want someone in on the ground floor, so to speak, at Majors. They're short of shopwalkers."

"*Shop*walkers, sir!"

"It's not a bad job," urged Rollison. "All you have to do is walk up and down being pleasant to people and keeping a watchful eye on the assistants."

Jolly lifted his chin.

"If you really think that it will serve any purpose I am perfectly willing to try," he said. "Will it be easy for me to get a post, do you think?"

"Yes," said Rollison. "Mr. Lund will put a word in with the temporary staff manager. Where is Mr. Lund now?"

"He went to visit his cousin," said Jolly.

"With police protection in very large boots," said Snub. "Nothing else has happened of interest here, you've had all the fun. There isn't likely to be a job for me at Majors, is there?"

Rollison grinned.

"Possibly," he said, "as an assistant—in Jolly's department."

"I think I can assure you that I should keep the stall in order," said Jolly dryly. "When shall I apply, sir?"

"I'll fix it as soon as I can," said Rollison. "Has there been any word from Grice?"

"None at all," said Jolly.

He went out, and Rollison shook his head at Snub in silent warning that he should not try Jolly too far. Then he gave his full attention to the remaining correspondence, which he had neglected for several days.

The front-door bell rang.

"Yes, sir," Jolly said clearly, "he has just finished luncheon, sir, and I am sure he will see you."

"Thanks," came Grice's voice, and a moment later Grice himself entered.

Rollison waved him to a chair and Jolly promptly brought in coffee, with two cups.

"Have some while you can," invited Rollison. "Jolly's going on holiday for a week or two."

"Jolly? Holiday!" exclaimed Grice.

"One would think him a slave," said Rollison reproachfully.

"He isn't far short," retorted Grice.

He was preoccupied or he would not have accepted that news so easily. He settled back in a chair, balancing his saucer on his knee, and began to talk. When Grice talked freely it was a sure sign that he was worried. His news was not good. There was no sign of Calvert, who had left his rooms in Hendon that morning, paid his landlady, and had his bags sent to the station at Waterloo. The bags had been collected before the police arrived, and the attendant at the cloakroom did not remember them or their collector. He had lived at Hendon for several months. The landlady did not know where he had lived before that. She admitted that he was a 'nice gentleman', but that she was often worried because he was out so late at night, and often away for several days and nights. He had never had a visitor at the house; there was no line at all to be picked up from there.

"Well, it's a pity," murmured Rollison.

"What do you make of it?" demanded Grice.

"Jekyll and Hyde," said Rollison quickly. "He spent only part of his time at Hendon. We want to know where he spent the rest. It was probably under a different name. Have you sent his photograph to the newspapers?"

"The only photograph I can get is one of him in a group at a Majors' dance," said Grice, "and it won't enlarge well, I'm afraid."

"I could touch it up," offered Rollison.

"That's an idea," said Grice promptly. "I'll have an enlargement or two taken and send 'em along." He finished his coffee. "I can't get much satisfaction out of Majors or Romeo about Calvert, either. He went there a year ago, straight from the Army, if what he said can be believed. No one knows why Romeo gave him the particular job."

"Romeo believes he can judge men at a glance," observed Rollison.

"That might be it, but I wouldn't like to be sure," Grice said. "Anyhow, he got the job, made a go of it for a few months and then began to pick the wrong men. It was about the time Calvert started picking people who made mischief among the staff that Romeo's holdings in Majors began to weaken. You know what happened to the shares." He paused, then added abruptly: "They're falling again today. They're down to seventeen and six for a pound share, and they should be up to thirty shillings if things were normal."

"Can't you trace the reason?"

"Someone's selling. I don't know who. It doesn't seem to be Romeo, but if he were unloading he wouldn't do it openly. I'll tell you one thing I have noticed," Grice added.

"What is it?" asked Rollison.

"There's a lot of buying in Ireland," Grice said. "Several large packets of Majors' shares have gone through Dublin brokers—the only really large packets that have been disposed of, most of them have come into the market in dribs and drabs. Did you know there was an Irish angle?"

Rollison murmured, "I know that Romeo's wife's just been there on a visit, and that someone sent her roses."

Grice stared.

"It's true. I gather that her parents live in Dublin," Rollison added, and rubbed his chin. "That might be interesting."

"What else do you know about Mrs. Romeo?"

"She's lovely but dumb."

"He married her only seven months ago," said Grice, "and *that* coincided with Calvert picking the wrong men, the shares falling and—"

"Peter Lund beginning to get worried!"

"Yes, that's true," said Grice. "Are you sure she's dumb?"

"I'm sure she sounded like it," said Rollison,

He told the detective all that had happened at Majors.

Grice confessed that he could make nothing of it. He had talked bluntly to Peter Lund, but Peter had not told him any more; Grice admitted that he did not think he knew anything else. Alice Hellier's statement seemed to be accurate. The gun which Rollison had taken from Calvert had been examined for prints, but none had been found. It was an Italian automatic, not registered in England, and there was no easy way of tracing its owner. Eventually Grice came back, as Rollison always did, to the fact that someone at Majors had helped Calvert in his plans to abscond; Grice did not doubt that Rollison was right when he said that Calvert had planned a getaway that day.

"Oh, there's an accomplice at Majors," Rollison said decidedly. "The little dark man who nearly came in, perhaps." He paused. "Hilary scared him away, you know. Hilary's a curious mixture of the naïve young man and efficient factotum."

"You mean, watch Hilary?"

Rollison laughed. "I certainly should! Are you putting any men inside Majors?"

"Two," said Grice. "They're new fellows, who won't be recognised by the store detectives."

"Thanks," said Rollison warmly, and Grice looked puzzled. "Then I don't see what else you can do," added Rollison, "except make sure that Peter and his cousin are closely watched. But I needn't worry about that, need I?"

"You need not," said Grice. "Well, I must be going. Er— Rolly."

"Yes."

"Is Jolly going to Ireland for his holiday?"

Rollison stared.

"Great Scott, no!" He chuckled. "But it's an idea. Won't the Irish police co-operate?"

"Oh, they co-operate, but it's not as if they were our own people," Grice said. "They say that Ireland's a good place to frolic in just now."

He laughed and opened the door. Jolly had already heard him moving, and was in the hall.

"Have a good holiday, Jolly," said Grice, and Jolly stared blankly at his departing back.

Except for Jolly, it was an uneventful afternoon. Grice sent the enlarged photographs of Calvert, and Rollison touched them up until he made them a true likeness of Calvert. He sent them back by special messenger. Soon afterwards, Peter arrived, looking clear-eyed and cheerful. He admitted that it had done him good to talk to Grice, and the knowledge that a policeman was following him all the time certainly helped. Alice was cheerful, and less worried, too, he said; astonishing nerve for a girl, hadn't she? Rollison agreed, and when Peter said that he ought to go to the office, told him of the plans for Jolly.

Peter's eyes shone.

"Great notion! And you're just the man, Jolly. You might find you like it better than being here, too."

"I beg leave to question the likelihood of that, sir," said Jolly.

"When can you engage him?" asked Rollison, from the depths of an easy chair.

"Come along and see me about four o'clock," said Peter. "Romeo will have put in a deputy staff manager by then, he never lets the grass grow under his feet. We'll fix you up!"

"Thank you, sir," said Jolly mournfully.

He was 'fixed up' by half past four. He returned to Gresham Terrace a little after five o'clock and crept silently about the flat until Rollison called for him. Jolly broke the news, and added: "As tomorrow is the first of the month, I was asked to commence my new duties then. I thought it advisable to agree, sir."

"It's a bit quick," said Rollison, "but I think it's wise. The first of April, Jolly!"

"Exactly, sir," said Jolly.

It took Snub less than a second to see the implications of that when he returned at half past five. There was some feeling between him and Jolly, and Rollison left them to work it out for themselves when he started out for Ligaro's Restaurant a little after half past six.

Hilary was late.

Because Rollison was known at Ligaro's, no one complained; the head waiter sympathised, and with his own plump hands brought and uncorked a bottle of Amontillado. He poured a little into a glass and tasted it, filled another glass which he handed to Rollison. His eyes shone.

Rollison sipped. "Wonderful!" he said.

"These people," said the head waiter. "Cocktails!" He raised his hands in despair. "M. Rolleeson will wait for a leetle while longer?"

"Another quarter of an hour," said Rollison.

The quarter of an hour was nearly up, and he had resigned himself to a solitary meal, and was already wondering why Hilary had not turned up, when Hilary entered the room. He stood on the threshold, gazing about him, showing all the signs of impatience. Then he saw Rollison and hurried towards him, completely ignoring the head waiter.

Rollison pushed his chair back.

Hilary drew up. "I've just had a message from Calvert!" he exclaimed. "That's what kept me."

Chapter Ten

Message From Dublin

"What kind of message?" asked Rollison.

Hilary dropped into a chair and passed his hand across his forehead. He was sweating, there was a glow of excitement in his eyes, and he was breathing heavily.

"The nerve of the fellow! He left some private papers in his desk, and wants me to post them to him."

"The police will have found them by now," said Rollison disappointedly.

"They won't have found these," declared Hilary. He leaned back in his chair and, to the dismay of the head waiter, took out cigarettes. Before dinner, that was an offence at Ligaro's. "They're tucked away in a secret compartment. He's told me just how to get at them. And—" Hilary hesitated.

"Go on," said Rollison.

"Damn his impudence! He said that if I didn't do what he told me, I'd be shot out of Majors inside a week!"

"*Did* he?" exclaimed Rollison.

"He always had the nerve of Old Harry," complained Hilary. "Can you order a whisky and soda?"

Rollison caught a glimpse of the head waiter, and picked up the Amontillado.

"Try some of this," he said, pouring out a glassful.

"Thanks." Hilary sipped, then widened his eyes. "By George!" He drained his glass and stubbed out his cigarette. "Sorry I'm a bit agitated," he said. "I was just about to leave my rooms when the telephone rang. Oh, I forgot to tell you—he's in Dublin."

"Oh, *is* he?" said Rollison.

"He wants me to send the things addressed to O'Brien, *posts restante*, Dublin."

"And you told him to go break his neck?"

Hilary laughed.

"I did! Then he weighed in with the threat about Majors and rang off before I had time to tell him what I thought. I don't know, of course," went on Hilary, "but I think my job at Majors is about as safe as anything can be. Still, that's by the way. The beggar sounded serious, you know, as if he really thought he could do something about it. You've already proved that he had an accomplice there, haven't you?"

"It's pretty evident," observed Rollison. "Have you told Romeo about this?"

"I haven't had time to tell a soul."

"And you haven't looked for the papers?"

"Now be your age," protested Hilary. "I've come straight from my rooms because I knew you were waiting here. If those papers are tucked away as Calvert says they are, they can stay there for a year without being found. And I—well, I wanted to talk to you. I'm all mixed up."

"We'll have to try to get you unmixed," said Rollison. He beckoned the head waiter, and went on, "Are you hungry?"

"Fairly."

"M'sieu," murmured the head waiter.

"Jules, we've been called away," said Rollison. "We hope to be back in about an hour. See that we're looked after, won't you?"

"Of course, m'sieu."

"Where—" began Hilary, holding back.

"Come on," urged Rollison,

The head waiter looked at Hilary with acute disfavour, and bowed to Rollison, who took Hilary's arm and led him past the crowded tables. They did not go unobserved. Outside, Rollison called out to a passing taxi which, to his gratification, pulled in. He bundled Hilary into the cab as he said to the driver: "Majors' stores; back entrance."

"Right, sir."

"What on earth has got into you?" demanded Hilary, leaning forward on his seat and peering through the darkness of the cab at Rollison. "What's the hurry?"

"Calvert's anxious for those papers. Therefore we should be. Someone else worked with Calvert at Majors and might know where the papers are."

"Oh," said Hilary, "I don't think there's any need to worry, but if you say so—"

They got out by the back door of Majors and Hilary rang the bell for the night-watchman as Rollison paid off the taxi.

Chapter Eleven

Secret Drawer

Their footsteps sounded clearly on the floor of the deserted, shadowy general office. A light was burning at the far end, just a dim glow which spread over several desks. As they neared the far end a telephone bell started to ring. Hilary jumped. The bell was on the far side of the office, and stopped as sharply as it had begun. The silence seemed more profound.

"Wrong number," murmured Rollison.

He led the way to the passage. As he neared it, he heard a rustle of movement. He stopped short, and Hilary cannoned into him. They stood with hearts beating fast, staring at the door. The movement stopped. Hilary muttered, "What was it?" Rollison did not speak but, keeping close to the wall, went nearer to the passage.

A door along it was open and light was shining out.

They stood still amid the gloom and the silence. The rustling sound came again, followed by a sharp click, as of a key turning in a lock. Rollison touched Hilary's arm, warning him to stay where he was, and peered along the passage. No one was in sight, but shadows of men were moving on the wall, cast by the light inside the office.

Rollison knew that someone was picking a lock. He made sure that the passage was empty before he stepped into it, whispering as he did so.

"You stay this side. I'm going to try to pass the door and get to the far side. If they're on the point of coming out we'll catch 'em between us."

"Oke."

They went forward silently, thankful for the carpet. Hilary stopped a yard from the open door and Rollison stepped swiftly past it. He glanced into the office. Two men were bending over Calvert's desk. Their faces were towards the door, but they were looking downwards. One of them was working at the lock, the other watching him.

Rollison passed the door safely and went to the corner—where, earlier in the day, a little dark man had run into Hilary and Williams and made his escape. No one was there; these two men had not stationed guards at either corner, so presumably they were alone. But were there any men outside on guard for them? It seemed likely. If there were, would they send a warning? Had that telephone call been for them? *Could* they send one? Rollison turned back from the corner, thinking swiftly. It was surely certain that the Yard had been alerted, so the police should be well on the way by now. There seemed little to fear from the men in the street. If they did make an attempt at warning, they would have to break into the store first.

How had these men broken in?

He put the question out of his mind, reached the door and peered inside again. The men were still absorbed in their work. One was nearly bald; the other was shorter, with a mop of dark, untidy hair. Rollison could see most of his swarthy face and his bushy eyebrows; was this *the* small dark man?

Rollison put his hand in his pocket, gripped his cigarette-case and held it against his coat, so that it looked as if he were carrying a weapon. He nodded to Hilary, whose eyes were bright with excitement.

Then Rollison turned into the office.

Neither man noticed him.

Hilary followed, but showed good sense by standing in the doorway and making no further move.

"Hallo," greeted Rollison politely.

The bald-headed man jumped so violently that he banged his hand on the desk and dropped his tools. Both of them stared at Rollison, their mouths agape. There was utter silence in the room, broken only by their heavy breathing. The dark man's hands were outstretched – large, long-fingered, prehensile hands which Rollison could not fail to notice. He was the first to recover from the shock. His mouth closed, he backed away a foot and dropped his hands. Rollison thrust the case sharply against the lining of his coat.

"I should keep them up," he warned.

The man kept them on a level with his shoulder.

The dark man said, "It's Rollison."

"With friends," said Rollison, "and others will be here very soon."

The dark man sprang at Rollison.

It was a prodigious spring. He dropped one hand to the desk and swung over it, coming bodily towards Rollison, his feet close together and driving at Rollison's chest. Rollison swung to one side. Hilary shouted. The bald-headed man rushed towards the door. Rollison waited until the dark man had nearly landed and then pushed him. The push, added to the momentum of the spring, sent him flying half-way across the office, and he fell heavily. Rollison reached him before he started to get up but the man kicked out at him. Rollison skipped aside. The dark man made another prodigious leap upwards, springing from his hands and knees. Rollison punched him on the nose, a blow with all his strength behind it. It hurt his hand, but it hurt the dark man much more. He sagged backwards and fell again; when he moved his head Rollison saw that blood was already streaming from his nose. Rollison went forward, pulled him to his feet and struck him on the side of the jaw. There came a half gasp, half groan, as his victim fell, spreadeagled on the floor.

"Grand work!" cried Hilary triumphantly.

He had the bald-headed man in a half-nelson, and was peering over the man's shoulder at Rollison. The bald-headed man was trembling with fear and his knees were wobbling. He could not keep his eyes from the man on the floor, and with his free hand he wiped his nose as if he were afraid that his was bleeding too. He had little round eyes and his eyelashes were so fair and thin that they appeared almost non-existent.

"What shall we do with him?" asked Hilary.

"I don't think he'll misbehave," said Rollison. "Stand him in a corner with his back to the wall."

The picker of locks was so relieved that he led the way to the corner, wincing when he pulled his arm too sharply in Hilary's grip. Rollison pushed a chair behind him, so that if he moved he would have to move the chair and thus arouse their attention. Then Rollison turned to the desk. He stood in front of it, listening for any sounds outside; there were none. Little noise had been made in the scuffle, and the night-watchman would not be on this floor for some time.

"Where did he say you would find these papers?" asked Rollison.

"There's a spring lock at the back of the top drawer," said Hilary. "I've got a master-key to the desk, I'll—" He half-turned, and then saw Rollison pick up the tool which the bald-headed man had been using and push it into the lock. "What are *you* going to do?"

"He's probably got it half open," Rollison said casually.

He twisted and turned. The bald-headed man stared at him with protruding eyes, and Hilary watched, fascinated. The narrow skeleton key caught the barrel of the lock; after several deft twists the lock clicked open.

"Good lord!" exclaimed Hilary.

"He's not even an expert at his job," said Rollison. "*I'd* better start giving the lessons. When the police come," he added, with a gleam in his eyes, "they'll know it was necessary to do this to make sure that the papers hadn't been stolen before."

"Oh yes!" said Hilary, grinning.

The man on the floor stirred. Rollison glanced at him, saw that he was still in a bad way, and pulled the drawer right out. There was very little in it – some cigarettes, a Ronson cleaning outfit, a diary and one or two odd papers. The police had obviously been satisfied that none of these was of any importance. Rollison went down on his knees and peered at the back of the drawer, beneath the knee-hole. He could not see clearly. He straightened up and took the desk-lamp and stood it immediately in front of the desk. The white light threw everything into sharp relief.

"Keep an eye on Darkie," he advised, for the man was stirring again.

On his knees, Rollison fingered the back of the desk. Nothing happened. He squatted down, hitched himself forward and examined it more closely. There was no sign of a spring. He moved his hand gently across the slots where the drawer fitted, putting his fingers well inside. In the left-hand corner he felt a tiny ridge. He pushed it right and left, but nothing happened. He pressed it with his fingernail against the ledge itself; the ledge fell back with a sharp sound.

"Any luck?" exclaimed Hilary.

"Yes. Don't forget Darkie," said Rollison.

He felt a rising excitement as he pulled the ledge farther down. There was a little cavity, about two inches deep by one inch high and twelve inches wide. It held a long scroll of papers. He took it out, dropped it, pushed it behind him and then hitched his way backwards. He nearly knocked the lamp over.

"Careful!" warned Hilary.

Rollison got to his feet and picked up the scroll. It was thick and fairly heavy; a great deal could be written there.

Darkie had regained consciousness.

He made no attempt to dry the blood which had streamed over his mouth and down his chin. He raised his head and stared, not at Rollison but at the scroll. He licked his lips and grimaced, and Rollison held the scroll up for his inspection,

"And what is the value of this little thing?" he asked cheerfully. "Any offers?"

The bald-headed man made a noise in his throat. The dark man got slowly to his feet. He was unsteady, and put out a hand against the wall. He watched Rollison closely, and Hilary chuckled and said: "Not for sale, eh?"

"I'll give you ten thousand pounds for it," said Darkie.

The words startled Hilary so that he drew in his breath sharply. The Toff took a firmer hold on the scroll. He watched the man, trying to make sure whether the offer had been made seriously.

"Ten thousand—*cash*," said Darkie.

"And where would you get the cash from?" asked Rollison.

"You needn't worry about that."

Hilary was staring at Rollison. "Look here, Rollison, you wouldn't dream of—"

"You shut up!" snapped Darkie. "Rollison, I'm serious. Ten thousand pounds in one-pound notes, where you like—but it must be some time tomorrow. I'll come to your flat for it if you like."

"I see," said Rollison. "But will the police let you out?"

The bald-headed man spoke in a shrill, unnatural voice.

"You can't turn it down! You can't! Ten thousand quid, and we haven't done any harm; you needn't tell the police!"

"But I had to tell them because you might have guards outside," said Rollison.

"*We* haven't got anyone outside. What d'you mean?"

"I don't know that I believe you" Rollison said. "Are you sure you didn't beat some friends or enemies by a short head, Darkie?"

Darkie said nothing, but his companion drew in his breath and stared at Rollison with increasing dismay. He licked his lips. Darkie growled, "Shut up, White!" But something was too clearly impressed on the other's mind for him to keep it to himself, and he exclaimed: "It's Rumble! It's Rumble, I tell you. He—"

"*Shut up!*" snapped Darkie.

"Do you know what they're talking about?" Hilary demanded.

Rollison shook his head.

"Had I better fetch one of the watchmen," Hilary asked, "or shall I stay?"

"That's an idea," said Rollison. If either of these men talked, it would be better if Hilary were not present, it might help them to talk more freely. "Don't be long," he added.

"I won't," promised Hilary.

Finding themselves alone with Rollison did not reassure either White or Darkie. Rollison stood looking at them, knowing they were increasingly afraid. White was more likely to crack.

He moved towards the man, who flinched.

"Don't worry, friend White," a man said from the doorway.

Rollison let the scroll fall to the floor and put his hand in his pocket – but the man in the doorway held a gun, and the threat of it made Rollison stand still.

Chapter Twelve

Rumble

"Rumble!" gasped the bald-headed man.

"Rumbled," said Rumble. He chuckled as he stepped farther into the room. He had been recognised by his voice, which had an accent Rollison could not place, certainly not from his face. He wore a hat pulled low over his eyes and a beard so false that it seemed to shriek the word aloud. He wore a raincoat and cotton gloves, and somehow looked well dressed. His voice was deep, and suited his name.

"I see you've managed to find Calvert's guilty possessions." said Rumble, and there was a laughing note in his voice. "That's saved me a lot of trouble. I wasn't quite sure where he kept them. Hand over."

"Later," said Rollison.

"Now," insisted Rumble. He held the gun loosely, but lifted it a shade. "This is a lethal weapon, you know, and it's loaded. Also, it has the latest thing in silencers attached. Listen."

He squeezed the trigger.

Rollison stood quite still. There was a soft hissing noise and a flash. The bullet buried itself in the wall behind Rollison's head.

"You see, it works," said Rumble. "Pick up the papers and throw them on the floor in front of me, Rollison. Don't be deceived by my lightness of manner—a lot of people have been, to their cost."

Rollison stooped and picked up the roll. He did not throw it at the bearded man, but looked at it with interest. Every eye in the room was turned towards it, and Rumble took a step forward; obviously the scroll mattered a great deal to him. Rollison put his head on one side and then dropped his hand to his waistcoat pocket; he took out his lighter.

"Rollison—" began the bearded man.

"I like to smoke in moments of tension," Rollison said. He flicked the lighter and applied it to the corner of the roll.

"Don't!" cried Rumble, and leapt forward.

Rollison struck him across the wrist with the roll. Rumble saw his mistake, shot out a leg, kicked and missed. Rollison snatched at the gun but missed it. Rumble jumped back …

Darkie and bald-headed White ran for the door.

"That's enough!" cried Rumble.

The flames had died down, the papers were too tightly rolled to burn. Rumble stood half-way between Rollison and the door, in complete control.

After a tense moment of silence Rumble motioned to Rollison again; and this time he would undoubtedly shoot if there were any attempt to trick him. Rollison weighed the roll in his hand, preparing to toss it, but before it left his fingers there was a shout from the passage.

"Look out!" That was White.

"*Go for them!*" That was Darkie.

"The police," said Rollison flatly, and tossed the roll on to the top of a steel cupboard; it disappeared from sight. Rumble looked at him and Rollison could imagine the anger in the eyes which were hidden by the brim of his trilby. But Rumble would not do murder while the danger was so great; he did not speak again, but backed out of the room and slammed the door. There had been a commotion outside, hardly noticed because of the tension in the office.

Rollison crossed to the door and opened it.

The commotion was in the general office and Rumble had turned right, towards the emergency staircase. Rollison went after him but as he reached the corner a bullet struck the wall near his head. He drew back. Rumble was standing by the open doors of the lift, covering Rollison. He backed into the lift and pulled the doors to.

Rollison did not move; the man with the gun was too dangerous. Not until it was out of sight did he make for the stairs, but he knew that there was no chance of catching Rumble; his hope was that the night-watchman or a policeman downstairs would stop the man. With hope there was anxiety; if Rumble were stopped he would try to shoot his way clear.

Rollison was on edge for the sound of shooting as he ran, but none came. The noise from the general office faded. He reached the ground floor some time after the lift had stopped; it was standing there with the doors wide open. There was a door to the street immediately opposite it, and the door banged in the wind. Rollison went to the street and looked right and left. Footsteps were fading in the distance.

He went back to the lift and pressed the fifth-floor button.

Bray had lost no time in calling Grice from his home, and an hour after the mêlée in the general office Grice was at Majors with the roll of papers in his hands. Bray stood behind him, rather pleased with himself, and not without reason.

Grice looked at the scorched end of the roll.

"Whose bright idea was that?" he demanded.

"Rollison's, of course," said Hilary, "and if it hadn't been for that Rumble would have got away with the papers."

Grice raised his eyebrows.

"And if Rollison hadn't insisted on coming here right away the others would have got it," said Hilary, determined that full justice should be done.

"What made you come here?" asked Grice.

Rollison told him briefly. Hilary sat back in a chair and listened with shining eyes. A plainclothes sergeant stood by the door while the other policemen were inquiring among the night-watchmen about the forced entry into Majors. That was preoccupying Rollison as he talked. Had any of the night-watchmen opened a door or made sure that one was left open?

That was less important, perhaps, than the papers.

"Well, aren't you going to look at them?" asked Hilary eagerly.

"Not yet," said Grice.

"It seems to me that you're wasting time," Hilary said impatiently. "You let Rumble—"

"'Let' is hard," said Rollison.

"Well, they should have watched all the doors," complained Hilary. "I'm fed up with footling questions while Rumble's wandering about London doing exactly what he likes."

"But without the papers," Rollison reminded him. "Bill."

"Yes?" said Grice.

"I'm hungry."

Grice laughed. "Then go and get some food!"

"Thanks. Let's go, Hilary," said Rollison, and silenced the youngster with a look.

A table in a secluded corner had been kept for them at Ligaro's. The head waiter, desolate because Rollison had rushed away, looked after them in person. He was gentler towards Hilary, who knew good food from bad and now showed a proper appreciation of the wine. Rollison talked idly about Romeo and Majors, leading Hilary on to talk, and he was conscious again of curious contradictions in Hilary's manner. He had been angry with Grice, but there was a hint of forced anger about it, as if he thought it had been politic to be annoyed but actually felt quite neutral. He talked freely. It soon became clear that he hero-worshipped Romeo, and, if he were any judge, so did Peter Lund. He and Peter got along famously, and were by way of being friends. Had Rollison met Peter's cousin?

"Alice?" asked Rollison.

"Yes." Hilary was very casual. "I met her once, and wondered how she was getting on. Nice girl."

"Attractive," murmured Rollison, and led the subject back to Romeo. "Not so attractive to look at as Mrs. Romeo, though."

"What? Don't be an ass!" exclaimed Hilary. "She'd make three of that painted doll. As I said this morning, I just can't understand anyone falling for a woman like that, especially Romeo. There's no accounting for taste. The trouble isn't with her *looks*," added Hilary, earnestly, "it's her mind. She hasn't got one in the true sense of the word. She's just vacant. Small talk dribbles out of her—if you can call it small talk. It worries me, because—well, Romeo's a brilliant man, you know, he's one of the coming men."

"He thinks he's arrived."

"He *says* he thinks he's arrived," said Hilary, and chuckled. "But no sooner does he get on top of one thing and he's off on another. He's talking of going into politics, and if he does he'll cause a stir! Still, politics don't affect this business. Er—I suppose you want to know what I think of Calvert and the position at the store?"

"Yes."

"It wouldn't surprise me if you don't know more than I do about some of it," said Hilary. He finished his coffee and lit a second cigarette. "All I know for certain is that there's some odd business going on behind the scenes, because Majors isn't rocky, although to look at the market prices of the ordinary shares and debentures you'd think we were." Rollison noticed the 'we'. "It's one of the soundest businesses imaginable, yet someone is trying to weaken it. The staff position is all mixed up in it, of course. I've often wondered why Calvert picked his losers. It *might* be just to make sure that the customers get fed up, so that the general reputation of the store suffers. But it beats me."

"Have you ever noticed that Romeo's worried?" asked Rollison.

"He doesn't say much. He *is* worried, of course; he can't make it out."

"Has he any personal worries?"

Hilary grinned.

"Only his wife, and he doesn't know about that one! He'll wake up to it one day. She's always flitting off here and there, pleasure-seeking, you know, and he hates her leaving him. Does it make any difference? No! She was on the stage for a while, but only just on," continued Hilary. "Chorus, by the skin of her legs, so to speak! She's been to see her people in Dublin three or four times since!"

"Just family love," suggested Rollison, lightly.

"It *can't* be!" cried Hilary. "It's too much to believe. And Grice was very interested in the Dublin angle. I say, Rollison, do you think there's anything in it?" He squashed his cigarette into a saucer and looked at Rollison with a hard light in his eyes. "If I thought that woman was playing Romeo for a fool—"

"Let's talk about that when we know she is," said Rollison, and looked at his watch. "I've got to go. Thanks for coming."

Hilary laughed. "Thank *you*!"

They parted outside, Hilary to go to his rooms in Bayswater, still agog with excitement, and Rollison to Ellerby Mews. He wanted to see Alice again, without quite knowing why. Grice's earlier suggestion that Calvert might have attacked her because of something which she knew and Peter Lund didn't carried weight. A quiet talk with her when there was no pressure of events would help him to form a clearer picture of her, and it would help him to keep back his curiosity about the papers.

There was a light at the door. The girl whom he had soothed the previous night opened it. Behind her stood a tall, sorrowful-looking young man. The girl was bright and merry. Oh, what a pity, but Alice wasn't in. She and Peter and a friend had gone off somewhere, followed by a *beastly* policeman. No, she had no idea where they had gone, and she didn't know the friend, who looked a pleasant young man.

Rollison left a message of greetings and walked back to Gresham Terrace. There was no holding his curiosity about the roll of papers now, and he wondered whether he should go to the Yard. He decided to telephone Grice in the hope that he would be more discursive without Hilary being present.

Jolly opened the door.

"Good evening, sir," he greeted. "I am very glad you are back, because Mr. Grice is waiting to see you."

Chapter Thirteen

Cause For Disappointment

All was not well.

Grice was standing up, looking unusually severe, as Rollison entered. Rollison waved him to a chair.

"No, thanks," said Grice. He turned to the desk and picked up a few sheets of paper which he had kept hidden until then. "You can have those back."

He dropped them on to Rollison's lap.

Each was scorched at the corner. Each was a small sheet of drawing-paper, covered with drawings which made Rollison widen his eyes. Several were sketches of heads and shoulders, some were of still life, and there were one or two crude attempts at drawing Venus de Milo with undue emphasis here and there. Rollison glanced at each one, conscious all the time of Grice's unfriendly gaze. Then he tapped them together and rolled them up carefully.

"No, thanks," he said.

"Where are the papers you took from the desk?" asked Grice.

"They *are* the papers. I recognise the scorching."

Grice sat on the corner of the table.

"You're not pulling anything, are you?" he demanded. "You don't seriously believe that men came and risked their freedom for those scribbles, do you?"

"There might be a code in them, you know, although the Cypher Department probably won't be able to make anything of them.

Either they do convey a message to someone or they had been planted in place of Calvert's original papers. But the only likely people to plant them, I should think, are Rumble and the other brace. They didn't, or they wouldn't have come for them. So—they mean something."

"I don't believe it," said Grice. "Did you recognise Rumble?"

"No." Rollison looked hopeful. "I think Darkie and White did."

"They won't say a word."

"I thought White was likely to crack," said Rollison.

"Something's stiffened him. Oh, he'll talk sooner or later, but it might be too late," Grice declared. "I'm becoming really worried about this business. I can't help feeling that you know more about it than you've admitted. If there is trouble with Majors, if they were to go broke, a lot of little people would suffer, you know, and there would be a big scandal. You don't want to get your fingers soiled with anything like that."

"No fear," agreed Rollison, warmly. "That's why I keep in closest touch with the police. May I make a suggestion? Send those papers – or good copies – to O'Brien, *poste restante*, Dublin. Send a message from Hilary with them. Have a man watching over there—or if you don't feel like taking a risk, let the Dublin police do it for you. We don't know anything about the papers except this: Calvert wants them and will probably take chances to get them."

Grice said, "I've already thought of it." He frowned, but there was a suspicion of a twinkle in his eyes. "*Are* you thinking of taking a trip to Ireland or sending Jolly over?"

"I might go," said Rollison. "But play fair. Will you send a man over too?"

"No, I'll work through the Dublin police," said Grice. "They'll be in the post tomorrow morning, wrapped in blue paper, and should get to the post office the morning after that."

When Grice had gone Jolly congratulated Rollison on putting him into an easier temper. Rollison laughed, and asked where Snub was. There had been a telephone call from Peter Lund, said Jolly, and Snub had gone to see him and Alice Hellier.

Rollison took a book of verse from his bookcase and read until gradually the cadence and gentle flow of the poetry took his mind off more pressing events; it was a good way to relax, often the only sure way. He was immersed in Belloc when he looked up with a start; the telephone bell was ringing. He heard Jolly cross to the main instrument in the hall, and cocked his head.

"This is the residence of Mr. Richard Rollison," said Jolly: "I—"

He broke off.

Rollison leaned forward and picked up the extension and heard Snub's voice; and Snub was excited.

"Tell him he must come, he mustn't lose any time. He *must*, Jolly!"

"To what address?" asked Jolly, without a sign of agitation.

Snub told him …

It was a house in Chelsea, away from the main roads, a small Georgian residence standing in its own grounds and clearly visible against the light of a waxing moon.

The house was in darkness.

Snub had telephoned from nearby, and had said that he would be on the look-out for Rollison, but there was no sign of him.

Snub had given no details, just made the urgent summons and rung off; Peter Lund and Alice had been with him, that was all Jolly knew.

As Rollison made his way towards the front door, across the top of which the porch cast a shadow, he felt annoyed with Snub.

He rang the bell.

No one came.

He walked towards the side of the house and then all round it, but no rooms were lighted. He tried several of the windows and found them fastened. Was this the right house? Had he taken the address wrongly from Snub? He went back to the end of the street, dissatisfied and worried, and made sure that he was right. His car stood in the main road, just out of sight from the house. He drove it nearer and then approached the house again; *Greengates, Hill Road, Chelsea,* and the gates *were* green. He approached the house and rang and knocked again. The echoes faded, but this time another sound broke the silence.

Someone was moaning.

The moans came softly. They came from inside the house, and after the first moment of alarm Rollison bent down and pushed the letterbox open. He could hear the moans more clearly. He dropped the box, which made a clattering noise, and then examined the lock. It was a Yale, and he had no tools with which to open it; and even with tools it would not have been easy. He hurried to the back of the house, to find a similar lock on the back door; but he found a casement window open an inch.

He managed to get the catch in the loop of a handkerchief, held swing fashion, and pulled it back. Once it was free, the window opened easily. He climbed in, letting himself down lightly to the floor. It was pitch dark on this side of the house, and he shone a pencil torch about the room. It shone on something bright; the taps of a hand-basin. He moved it slowly, and the beam fell upon the door.

Outside was a passage.

Then the moaning started again.

The sound was low-pitched, more sigh than moan, and it came from the direction of the pale light. He went quickly along the passage, shining his torch until he saw electric switches. He pressed one down, and a good light flooded a large hall, richly carpeted and as richly furnished. The soft, sighing sound continued; it was almost as if someone was trying to play on his nerves.

Two doors opened from the passage.

He pushed one open wider and stepped inside. The sighing became louder. He switched on the light; concealed wall lighting showed every corner of a drawing-room, exquisitely furnished in Louis Quinze style. The carpet was of duck-egg blue, the decor was maroon and that same pale blue. It was a lovely room; a setting fit for a lovely woman, but its beauty was slashed by the ugliness which lay upon the floor.

A man, lying face downwards, with arms stretched out and legs twisted, lay in a patch of browny-red blood which had come from his face and neck. He was quite still. Near him on the floor, leaning against a chair, was Alice Hellier; and she was uttering that sighing, moaning sound which brought horror to the scene.

The man was Peter Lund.

The girl was unconscious, and moaning as if she were coming round from gas or chloroform.

Rollison stood motionless for what seemed a long time, then moved swiftly. He went on his knees beside Peter, and raised his head gently; his fingers were stained with blood. He did not need to examine him too closely; Peter's eyes were open and glazed; he was dead.

Rollison let his head down again gently, then turned to Alice. There was a faint smell of chloroform at her mouth but she was not otherwise hurt. He took cushions from a settee and made her comfortable, then stood up and looked about him. In a corner a telephone was partly covered by a Dresden shepherdess. He covered his blood-stained hand with a handkerchief and lifted the telephone, to make sure that any fingerprints were not smeared, then dialled Scotland Yard. The girl had stopped moaning again and was lying limp with her head on her chest. The brisk, confident voice of the Yard operator was welcome …

"Give me Superintendent Grice's office, please."

"One moment, sir."

Rollison held on, trying to think clearly, asking himself senseless questions.

"Grice speaking," said Grice, briskly.

"Hallo, Bill!" Rollison was buoyed up at the sound of that assured voice. "You ought to be at home!"

"You *again*," said Grice, heavily.

"With much more trouble," said Rollison. "I'm at *Greengates, Hill Road, Chelsea*. Peter Lund has been killed here—"

"What?" cried Grice.

But Rollison, looking out of the window into the moonlit road, saw a car pull up outside the house, and noticed, the tiny lights of the sidelamps.

"Hurry!" added Rollison, abruptly. *"Greengates, Hill Road, Chelsea."*

He rang off, watching the car.

Chapter Fourteen

Poor Peter

A man opened the front gate.

It was too late for Rollison to switch off the light, whoever was coming had seen it by now. It was a man in a peaked cap and a dark uniform – a chauffeur. He stood by the gate and another man appeared with a woman by his side.

Romeo and his wife were coming here!

Rollison stepped to the wall and looked out of the window so that he could not be seen. He could hear Romeo speaking, but did not catch what he said. He opened the window an inch, and immediately the fat man's booming voice reached his ears.

"Go and see who it is, Harold! Go at once!"

"Yes, sir," said the chauffeur.

The man walked smartly up the path, while Romeo stood with one arm about his wife's shoulders. Next moment the sound of a key grating in the lock came clearly.

"You wait out here, my dear," boomed Romeo, and left his wife's side.

Rollison crossed the room and stood behind the door.

The two men reached the door. Rollison heard their exclamations, the chauffeur's a rough oath, Romeo's a shrill cry. They stood quite still.

"W—w—what—" began Romeo, and then his voice faded.

"You'd better not let madam see it, sir," said the chauffeur. He stepped forward, looking cautiously about him but forgetting to look behind the door. Rollison saw his broad face and horrified eyes. Then Romeo tiptoed in, and from outside there came the sound of footsteps on the path, followed by a shrill cry from Chloe.

"Is anyone there? Gus! Have you found anything?"

"Don't—don't come in for a moment, my dear!" boomed Romeo, and his voice took on a new resonance. "Wait just a minute!" He lowered his voice; clearly he had got over the first shock, perhaps anxiety for his wife had helped him. "Harold, who is it?" he asked in a whisper. "Who—?"

"It *looks* like Mr. Lund, sir," said Harold.

They could not know that anyone was behind the door; Rollison was getting their true reaction, and they were surprised as well as shocked; they knew nothing about this crime. He moved forward. Romeo was now in the room, a foot or two ahead of him, and the chauffeur was on his knees beside the body. Romeo was looking towards Alice; he raised his hands in alarm, then moved quickly towards her.

"I shouldn't touch anything," Rollison advised.

The chauffeur started so wildly that he lost his balance and fell against a chair. Romeo went stiff, but only turned his head. The chauffeur recovered and jumped up, then snatched at a chair and raised it, ready for action. Romeo recognised Rollison, blinked, and turned round slowly.

"*Well*, sir?"

"I shouldn't touch anything," repeated Rollison, "because the police will soon be here and you might confuse them." He took out cigarettes and offered them to Romeo, who took one with fingers which were a little unsteady. Then he offered one to the chauffeur, who backed away and demanded in a high-pitched voice: "Do you know him, sir?"

"Yes, Harold, you may put the chair down," said Romeo. "You always choose the right moment to appear, Mr. Rollison." He accepted a light. "Thank you."

"*Gus!*" Chloe Romeo was now in the porch, and her voice was trembling with agitation.

"I'll be with you in a moment, precious, stay there!" called Romeo.

"*Who are you talking to?*"

"Don't worry for a moment, my dear," called Romeo, anxiously.

"I had an SOS, and found all this," said Rollison, "and I telephoned for the police. How long have you been out?"

"A little more than two hours," said Romeo.

"Where have you been?"

"Really!"

"Someone would like you blamed for this murder," Rollison said, "and unless you're ready with your answers when the police come, you might find yourself in a cell tonight." He sat on the arm of a fragile-looking chair, and smiled at Romeo. "Does anyone know where you've been?"

"I have been out."

"With friends?"

"On my own—except for my wife."

"And chauffeur?"

"He—he picked me up half an hour ago," said Romeo. "Rollison, I will not stand here and listen to your ridiculous innuendos. I will not have it! Harold! Telephone the Dorchester—"

"I don't want to get rough," said Rollison, "but you're not going to use that telephone until the police have finished with it." Neither of the others defied him. "So you've been out, Romeo, alone with your wife, and no one can say that you were out of the house when the murder was committed. Is that right?"

Romeo blinked.

"Yes, that is right." He looked at Peter Lund, then shrugged his shoulders. "I see what you mean. Harold, perhaps it will be wiser if we do not telephone for a little while. But I *must* go and reassure my wife." He disappeared, moving with long, silent strides, and soon his voice boomed out. "There has been a little accident, my dear—"

"Little accident!" exclaimed Rollison.

The chauffeur made no comment; he was looking at Rollison warily.

Alice began to moan again.

The sound was louder, and Rollison crossed to her. She stopped moaning, and opened her eyes very wide. In that moment awareness of danger seemed to return, as if she felt fear – probably her last emotion before she had lost consciousness. She stared up into Rollison's face; then her head moved and she looked towards Peter. It was too late for Rollison to get between her and the body. She stared at it, and her lips grew taut; he could see the muscles of her neck tighten, too. Her hands clenched, and suddenly tears flooded her eyes. She uttered no sound, but sat there staring as the tears rolled down her cheeks.

"Let me help you up," said Rollison quietly.

She let him help her to her feet, but she did not seem to care whether she was sitting or standing. Rollison led her out of the room. The hall light was still on. Romeo was talking in a booming whisper. But his wife saw Rollison and the girl, and exclaimed: "Who's that?"

"Honey, you must go to the Dorchester," pleaded Romeo; "you mustn't worry, and—"

Chloe broke away from his restraining hand and hurried into the hall. She stared at Alice, whose face was still wet with tears.

It was an odd moment.

The lovely creature was tense with excitement laced with fear, but something seemed to flow into her as she looked at Alice. She came forward more slowly, with one hand outstretched.

"What *is* the matter?" she asked.

Rollison said, "Mr. Lund has been killed, Mrs. Romeo, and his cousin—"

"Rollison!" cried Romeo.

His wife's eyes widened. She looked past Rollison into the room. She could see the body on the carpet. She raised her hands and drew in an involuntary breath, but that was the only sign of alarm that she showed. She took Alice's arm and spoke in a gentle voice.

"You poor dear. And poor Peter Lund!" She looked at Rollison. "I will look after her, Mr. Rollison. Come upstairs with me, dear," she added and, putting an arm about Alice's shoulders, led her to the wide staircase.

Romeo stared at her as if he could not believe his eyes.

"You never know until you try," murmured Rollison. "She'll be all right. Where is your staff?"

"Out—out for the night," said Romeo. He licked his lips and watched the two women disappearing on the landing. "I would never have believed she had the—the courage!" he exclaimed.

"Some hothouse flowers grow in chilly weather," Rollison observed. "So the servants are away—you sent them away, did you?"

"That is *my* business!"

"The police will make it theirs," said Rollison, dryly, "but be awkward if you like."

Then a car drew up outside the house, and from it Grice came hurrying to the door with a doctor, Bray, and a sergeant in attendance. A second car-load of policemen followed.

Romeo stiffened; he stared towards the policemen, then spoke in a whisper only just loud enough for Rollison to hear.

"Some drawings—very amateur—most important—remember that." He strode forward with his hands outstretched and his lips set in a smile of welcome. "Superintendent!" he boomed. "How good of you to come so quickly!"

Grice said, "The matter is urgent."

Chapter Fifteen

'Buy!'

Grice interrogated Romeo with such astuteness that Rollison listened and looked on with increasing admiration. Romeo was constantly on the defensive but always firm in declaring that he knew nothing of Peter's death; nor had he known that Peter was coming to the house. He had been out to take a walk across the common at Wimbledon, he said, a walk which he and his wife often took. The chauffeur had dropped them at Putney Heath, by the Green Man, and picked them up an hour and a half later, If Grice did not believe that such walks were a regular feature of his life, a great number of people would vouch for them.

The chauffeur had stayed near the Green Man all the time.

Yes, Romeo admitted, there *had* been time for him and his wife to get back to the house, kill Lund and get away again, but they had not done so. Lund was a most promising young man; he had a great regard and affection for him; the thought that he might have killed the young man was preposterous. He could not answer for the activities of the murderer; respectfully, he suggested that it was a matter for the police, and the police had good reason to know that Peter was in some danger. Wasn't it a fact that the police had been watching Peter – acting, as it were, as a bodyguard?

That was the first time he discomposed Grice.

Grice was non-committal and, in front of Romeo and his wife, questioned Alice. All she told them was that Peter had received a call he *thought* came from Romeo, to see him at the house at half past nine. He had telephoned to Rollison, but had spoken to Snub, who had hurried to join him. Peter, Snub and Alice had left to keep the appointment, and Snub had stayed outside. The other two had been admitted by a manservant and taken into the sitting-room. All Alice remembered after that was a sack being dropped over her head and a sweet, sickly, overpowering smell. She had lost consciousness and not come round until she had seen Rollison – and, beyond him, Peter.

Her voice was harsh with repressed emotion, but she did not break down again.

Chloe Romeo stood by her side throughout the questioning. Chloe's manner and poise might have persuaded Hilary to revise his opinion of her.

Half-way through the second interrogation of Romeo, Grice turned to Chloe.

"I wonder if you will take Miss Hellier upstairs again?"

"Yes, of course," said Chloe.

Romeo, Grice, Rollison and Bray went into a small room next to the drawing-room, leaving the chauffeur in the hall with a police sergeant. Bray sat in a corner with a notebook open on a table, taking shorthand notes.

Bray put down his pencil and rubbed his fingers together to ease the cramp. Grice looked frowningly at Rollison, who held his peace. Romeo was permitted to go and telephone the Dorchester.

"What brought you here?" asked Grice, abruptly.

"An SOS from Snub Higginbottom."

"Where is he now?"

"That's my chief worry," said Rollison grimly.

"What did he tell you?"

"Only that I was wanted here. You can be pretty sure that Peter wasn't dead at the time of the telephone call," Rollison went on, "and that was at ten minutes to eleven. Does that agree with the doctor's opinion?"

"He said between nine and eleven o'clock, probably nearer eleven," said Grice. "Are you sure you don't know where Higginbottom is?"

"Haven't we had enough doubts about my good faith?" asked Rollison, without rancour. "I'm doing everything I can, Bill, and I've nothing up my sleeve."

"Has Romeo told you anything else?"

Rollison leaned forward.

"Yes. He's interested in some childish drawings. If I were you I'd show the same admirable restraint and postpone mentioning that to him just yet. There's more in Romeo than meets the eyes, and plenty meets the eye! There's more in his wife than I thought, too."

Chloe Romeo asserted herself again, not half an hour afterwards, when Romeo told her that he had booked rooms at the Dorchester. Why should she run away from her own home? Why shouldn't she stay, as only the drawing-room was wanted by the police? She intended to stay; and she hoped that the poor child would stay with them for the night.

"I don't think that would be wise," Rollison said, and Romeo looked at him gratefully.

"I—I don't want to go back to the flat," Alice said, in a nervous voice. "My friend will be out for the night, and—"

"I won't leave you alone," Rollison promised.

After a word with Grice he decided to take Alice to the Marigold Club, which was not at all what it sounded: it was a hostel for the wealthy. Lady Gloria Hurst, an aunt of Rollison's, not only had rooms there but had much say in its affairs.

He drove off with Alice sitting beside him and a police car following; the police would watch the Marigold Club, and that, Rollison thought, was a good thing.

Chapter Sixteen

A Visit From Romeo

Rollison woke up next morning to an unaccustomed silence.

It was a quarter to nine.

He got up, calling, "Jolly!" There was no answer. Only when he saw the kettle on a low gas in the kitchen, the breakfast-table laid, toast in the rack and newspapers and the post by the side of his plate did Rollison remember that it was April the first. Jolly had gone to business.

He glanced at the newspapers.

They had not yet got the story of Peter's murder, but they had a good account of what had happened at Majors in the morning and during the night. Romeo was featured prominently in all of them, and his photograph appeared in most. The *Daily Wire* had a photograph of Chloe at her loveliest, and had also managed to get one of Alice Hellier to put beside Peter's – Peter, having won fame during the war, was still news. There was nothing startling in any of the newspapers except one story of the remarkable unpopularity of Majors' shares on the market.

At ten o'clock Grice telephoned. The detective officer who had followed Lund had been killed in a car crash the previous night, and his body had been so mangled that he had not been identified for some hours. There was no news of Snub, said Grice, but the police were now searching high and low for him.

Aunt Gloria telephoned to say that Alice was sleeping the sleep of exhaustion, and had Rollison any requests to make about her?

"Keep the police away from her as long as you can," said Rollison. "Get a doctor to swear that she mustn't be worried, if needs be."

No sooner had he finished speaking than Hilary came on the telephone. Was there any truth in the rumour that Peter had been murdered? He had seen it in a Stop Press ... Good lord! ... Shocking! ... That probably explained the sharp drop in Majors' shares, they were down to fourteen shillings and threepence and it looked as if they were going to fall lower.

"I was afraid of that," said Rollison. "If you've got any money, buy."

"*Buy?*"

"Buy," repeated Rollison. He rang off immediately, and telephoned his brokers. Yes, there was a run on Majors, which amounted to a slump.

"Buy," said Rollison, briefly.

"*Buy?*"

"As hard as you can," said Rollison. "Sell out as much as you like of my other stuff, and buy."

"You must be mad!"

"I'm not mad at all," said Rollison. "Buy, old chap—don't risk too much of other people's money, though."

"Look here, if you buy big at the start you'll stop the fall."

"That's what I want to do. It hasn't reached the fringes yet; the small holders won't think of selling shares until the bottom's dropped right out of them, and I want to keep the bottom in. I am *not* crazy," Rollison assured him. "Buy!"

"Oh well," said the broker.

Grice was on the telephone again at twelve o'clock. After a weak opening and a sharp slump, Majors' shares had steadied and were even recovering a little. Did Rollison know who was buying?

"I am," said Rollison.

"I suppose you know what you're doing," Grice said.

"Listen to me, William! It will soon become known that I'm buying big and stopping the fall, and whoever wants that fall will come after me. Got the point?"

"I think I'd better have you watched," said Grice slowly.

"Please yourself," said Rollison. "Don't forget I'm going to Ireland this evening. Is there any news of Snub?" he added, without much hope.

"None at all, I'm afraid," said Grice.

"Rumble?"

"We can't trace the man," said Grice, "and Darkie and White still refuse to talk. I shall have another go at Romeo during the day."

"Let him sweat," advised Rollison. "Wait until we see what happens in Dublin at the very least."

He was thinking of Snub when the front-door bell rang and he hurried to answer it, hoping that Snub would be there. He saw a wide-brimmed hat through the frosted glass of the door. 'Not Snub,' he thought, and opened the door.

"Good afternoon," said Chloe Romeo.

Rollison covered his surprise in a delighted: "Why, hallo! Come in."

"Thank you very much," said Chloe. She swept in, a really lovely creature with a wonderful grace of carriage. "I *am* glad you're in, I so want to talk to you."

"Will you have some tea?" asked Rollison hospitably.

"Oh no, it's much too early for tea yet," said Chloe. "Mr. Rollison, how *is* that poor child? It's a strange thing, but she's very much like a girl I once saw with that dreadful man Calvert."

"Oh," remarked Rollison, watching his visitor closely.

"My husband won't have it, but *I* think that Calvert's behind all this—all this *mystery*," said Chloe. "What I really came about was Alice Hellier, though. Is Miss Hellier far away?"

"Not so very far," answered Rollison.

"I've been to her flat and to poor Peter Lund's home, but she's at neither place," said Chloe. "I'm *so* anxious about her. I feel that I could *help* her, Mr. Rollison."

"Perhaps you will be able to," said Rollison. "You can take it from me she's quite safe, comfortable and well looked after."

"That's *such* a relief! Well, thank you very much," said Chloe. "I am grateful. I—"

The front-door bell rang.

"Who's that?" exclaimed Chloe.

"I have a lot of callers," Rollison reassured her. "I won't keep you long."

He left her in the drawing-room, standing by the door and watching him, and walked across the hall. She had puzzled him from the beginning and mystified him now. She *wasn't* quite real; what woman, on so brief an acquaintance, would have confided in him like that – not under the stress of any emotion but as coolly and calmly as if she were talking without real thought?

This time a big figure showed through the glass.

He glanced over his shoulder quickly. Chloe disappeared when she saw him move. Perhaps his expression had warned her whom to expect.

Romeo stood on the threshold.

Here was a different Romeo, pale-faced, hard-eyed, angry. He stepped forward, pushing Rollison aside, and he did not sneak. He strode towards the open door of the drawing-room and would have stalked inside had Rollison not caught up with him and gripped his arm. Rollison's fingers sank deep in the flabby flesh, and Romeo winced but tried to pull himself free. Rollison's grip tightened.

Romeo half-turned. "Let me go!" His voice was hoarse with anger.

Rollison said, "What the devil do you think you're doing?"

Romeo said, "I have come for my *wife*, Rollison."

Again he tried to pull himself free and was surprised when he failed. He seemed impatient of the delay, and shook his arm much as a dog might shake himself to be free of something caught in his fur. He was looking towards the open door, and there was hardness in his eyes and at his mouth.

"What makes you think your wife is here?" demanded Rollison.

"I *know* she is here. Let me go!"

Rollison said, "You've been misinformed, and—"

Romeo raised his free hand and swung his arm, striking at Rollison's face. It was a powerful blow, that of a man swatting an elusive mosquito, and Romeo's manner was much as if he were dealing with an irritating but relatively unimportant interlude. Rollison swayed to one side but could not dodge the blow completely. It hurt his cheek. He countered with a jab to Romeo's stomach. His fist sank in. Romeo gasped with pain, belched and staggered away,

Rollison let him go.

Romeo backed to a chair, knocked against it and almost fell. He was staring at Rollison as if he could not believe that this had happened to *him*.

"You—you—you *struck* me!"

"Now you know what it's like," said Rollison sharply. "What makes you think your wife is here?"

"I received—I received a report."

"From whom?"

"Rollison, this is *my* business—"

"This is my flat and you've made too free of it," said Rollison, still sharply. "Do you mean that you have your wife watched?"

Romeo gulped. It was easy to see that he was now thinking quickly, that he realised he had overshot the mark and would find Rollison difficult. He closed his lips and began to rub his stomach gingerly. There was no other sound in the flat, and Rollison wondered what Chloe was thinking of all this – or whether she had expected it. At last Romeo said: "I—I am sorry, Rollison. I forgot myself. I am really sorry. I am so—so worried about my wife. Since I was warned that she—she might be hurt, I have been really frightened."

"Who warned you? The man who telephoned you yesterday?"

"Yes," said Romeo, "yes."

"What did he say?"

"That—that I must not accept *your* help."

Rollison said sharply: "So he knew that I was with you in the office. Was it Calvert?"

Romeo gaped. "I—"

Rollison said slowly: "Romeo, you told me about a man who was carrying on a vendetta against you. That was only partly true. Let's have the whole truth now."

"I— It *is* true. A man—"

Rollison snapped: "You mean that Calvert was blackmailing you. That's why you let him stay as staff manager; that's why, when he told you he had to leave because of something that had happened the previous night, you agreed to let him take the wages money— you *had* given instructions, Romeo, you knew what was going to happen. And after he'd fled he telephoned to try to prevent me from working with you. Isn't that the truth?"

There was a long, tense pause.

Romeo sat on the arm of a chair.

"Yes," he sighed. "Yes, that is all true. Calvert is the man of whom I spoke. He has carried on a bitter feud, he has blackmailed me, he—*he* is responsible for the trouble with Majors. He had influence with large shareholders; they are unloading. Calvert is buying some shares in Dublin or through a Dublin agent, and when they reach bottom he will buy heavily. He wants to ruin me, Rollison."

Rollison said slowly, "Why don't you buy?"

Romeo stood up and raised his hand.

"Every penny of my capital is in Majors," he declared. "If the store fails I shall fail. I have not spared a penny. I believed I should reap the reward—until Calvert came. He came with the hand of friendship extended and I thought that bygones were bygones. *Now* I know better. Not until this morning, when he disclosed his real purpose, did I realise it. You are quite right in all you have deduced, but I would rather lose everything than see my wife hurt. For that reason only I asked you to take no further part in my affairs."

"I see."

"I have her closely watched, for her own safety, and I heard she had come here," said Romeo. "I was afraid that she, out of the goodness of her heart, wanted to tell you what she could—part of this story. And then—" He dropped his hands and looked at Rollison helplessly. "I am hardly responsible for what I do where my wife is concerned; I suffer from waves of uncontrollable jealousy. When I came here I was thinking of—of your reputation as a lady's man, and—*do* forgive me, Rollison, please. *Is* my wife here?"

Rollison said slowly: "She has been. She came to inquire about Alice Hellier."

"Oh," said Romeo. "I see. That poor child. Chloe has deep chords of sympathy. I know, I know. I hate myself for my behaviour sometimes." He essayed a wan smile "In all other respects I am a normal man, Mr. Rollison, but Chloe—"

He closed his eyes.

Rollison heard a rustle of movement, turned, and saw Chloe coming into the room. She was smiling radiantly. She raised a hand with her fingers at her lips. Rollison shrugged his shoulders resignedly. When she reached him she whispered: "It is all right now."

Romeo opened his eyes.

"*Chloe!*"

"Hallo, precious," said Chloe brightly; "you *are* a silly old thing ..."

He had to be at London airport at half past six, and at five-twenty-five Jolly arrived. Rollison had brought the car round to the flat. Jolly looked tired, and Rollison drove; Jolly would drive the car back. The day had been interesting but unusual, he reported. There had been so much excitement over the trouble at Majors and the news that Peter Lund had been murdered that the staff had forgotten to be impolite and had behaved naturally. There were some signs of dissatisfaction, said Jolly, but he could not place his finger on the real reason for it yet.

Chapter Seventeen

Greeting At Dublin

"You can unfasten your belts and smoke if you would like to," said the hostess and then knelt down by the side of a nervous passenger and started to talk cheerfully. There was practically no wind, it would be the smoothest of trips, weren't they lucky? Rollison smiled as he saw the woman's anxious expression ease, and then stared at the back of Hilary's head. The man was four seats in front of him, and, unless he walked up to the toilet cabin at the end of the aircraft, would not see him.

Should he reveal himself?

Rollison decided not to.

He had spoken to Hilary on the telephone during the afternoon, and the youngster had not mentioned that he was going to Ireland. Had he received last-minute instructions from Romeo?

The aircraft flew steadily, with hardly a quiver. They had reached seven or eight thousand feet, and the lights of London had already merged together in soft haze behind them.

Rollison's taxi was a powerful Chrysler, the sight of which gave him hope. The driver was a young fellow with a rich accent, who put the suitcases on the seat next to him and demanded :

"Where to, sor?"

"Did you see the car which left just now?" asked Rollison.

"That I did."

"Try to catch up and follow it," said Rollison.

"So it's like that, is it, now?" exclaimed the driver. "We'll be after him, then!" He let in the clutch and the car moved off swiftly, swung right out of the airfield and hummed along the main road. It was some time before the rear-light of a car ahead showed through the darkness, but five minutes later the taxi had passed it.

"'Tis the right one, sor!"

"Yes. Let it pass as soon as you can," said Rollison.

The driver turned and winked.

A flood of cyclists, three trams and several private cars gathered near Trinity College conspired to beat him. The big car slipped ahead and disappeared. The taxi-driver cursed himself and the cyclists, the trams and the cars, the weather and the drivers of the private cars, and then said that he thought he knew where the other car was going.

"It'll be the Royal Hibernian, sir; there wouldn't be any reason to go this way for anything else; they'd go round O'Connell Street for the Gresham. What shall I do if it's outside, sor?"

"Pull in behind it and wait," said Rollison,

They slowed down outside the Royal Hibernian, but there was no sign of Hilary or the car which had brought him from the airport. The driver took both hands off the wheel and complained to the world at large. Rollison took it philosophically, since there was nothing else to do, paid his man generously and watched the grey-haired night porter walking up the steps of the hotel with his suitcase.

He followed slowly.

It was possible that Hilary had seen him and hurried out of the car; he might deliberately have gone to a different hotel when he realised which way Rollison was heading; but Rollison did not think he had been recognised. Nevertheless, he went to the main lounge cautiously, looking out for Hilary. The porter called him to the reception desk.

A tall, thin, smiling girl greeted him pleasantly.

"Good evening, sir. Have you a reservation?"

"Yes—Rollison." Rollison glanced at the hoard on which was written in chalk the names of residents for whom messages were waiting. He did so casually as the girl looked down her list; and he saw his own name written clearly.

A message from Jolly, perhaps? Or Grice—

"Yes, sir," said the girl, "room number eighteen. There's a message for you, I *think*." As he signed the register she looked for the message and took out an envelope. "Thank you, Mr. Rollison. I hope you have a pleasant stay in Dublin."

"Thanks very much," said Rollison, mechanically.

He was looking at the envelope and his heart leapt; for the handwriting was unmistakably Snub's.

"Thanks very much," he repeated more warmly. "Did you see the man who brought this?"

"I'm sure I didn't, sir, he would have given it to the porter—and the porter's off duty now, I'm afraid; we've changed over for the night."

"Never mind," said Rollison. He felt immeasurably cheered.

A page-boy took him to his room – a small double room, comfortably furnished. The lights were dim. He stood beneath one and read three lines written in Snub's clear, neat and unmistakable hand. It was characteristic of Snub:

> *Welcome to Ireland! The food's A1. I'm staying round the corner. So is a merchant who I think is named Rumble. Ever heard of him? S.*

The grill came and Rollison set to. He finished with a cream meringue and coffee, lit a cigarette and looked about the dining-room, which had emptied save for a dozen people. It was after ten o'clock.

Then the door from the lounge opened and a couple stood looking down. The woman was fat and middle-aged, and the man …

He was Rumble, complete with beard.

Chapter Eighteen

Work For Snub

He was smiling and showing white teeth beneath his beard. His hair was dark and curly, like the beard, and now that he was not wearing a hat the beard seemed more real than false. That was odd. Rollison looked towards him blankly, the waiter put the bill on a plate and hurried off.

"Hallo, Rollison!" exclaimed Rumble, cheerfully.

"Hallo," said Rollison, cautiously.

"Surely you recognise me," said Rumble. His eyes were rather bloodshot, but looked merry. He pulled up a chair and sat down. "We met last night, at Majors. I know this is a shock," went on Rumble, "but *I* have no ill-feelings. It's my bad luck that you have come into this affair."

"Too bad," drawled Rollison.

"Cheer up! You might get some bad luck before it's over."

Rumble lit a cigarette, and the little cylinder looked absurd against the great beard. "I always thought you were a cheerful chappie, Rollison, and not easily put out. Don't destroy one of my boyhood illusions."

"Are you as young as all that?" asked Rollison.

Rumble chuckled.

"That's more like it! Yes, I was at school when I first hero-worshipped the Toff! Odd life, isn't it? I didn't think we should ever be on different sides of the counter, but—well, we'll have to make the best of it. Won't you join me?"

"I've finished, thanks."

"Come and have coffee," urged Rumble. "We may as well remain friends while we can. And there's someone you'd like to meet, I think."

"A friend of yours?"

"My mother."

Rollison watched him narrowly.

"And, naturally, my sister's mother," said Rumble.

He saw the mystification in Rollison's eye, and chuckled with boyish delight. He *was* young, perhaps in his middle twenties. It was the beard that made him look older. And he was intent on increasing Rollison's uncertainty. His mother—his sister's mother …

Chloe Romeo's parents lived in Dublin.

"What a pity the whole family isn't here," murmured Rollison. "But Chloe only went home yesterday morning, didn't she?"

"Well done!" exclaimed Rumble. "I thought I'd get you all mixed up. Between you and me, I've no time for Chloe. It's a sore point with the old girl. She is equally fond of us both, but Chloe and I always fight like cat and dog—and I suppose we always shall. Now I have no time for any woman who marries a pig like Romeo."

"Pig?"

"Swine, if you prefer it. I like 'pig'. Have you ever seen him eat?"

"I've seen him drink."

"Oh, he has a semblance of culture," said Rumble, carelessly. "Won't you come over?"

"I'm afraid I've a pressing appointment," said Rollison,

"So soon? With the telephone, perhaps, to tell your friends the police that you have discovered me in Dublin. But I don't think extradition will be very easy, you know. I am Irish by birth and have never changed nationality. In Ireland they are jealous of their citizens. Besides, identification wouldn't be easy. I like to wear this beard because it amuses me and others, but without it …" He put his hand to his ear.

"Don't tell me it's false," said Rollison. He thought that in an excess of confidence the man might take the beard off, but Rumble simply chuckled and took his hand away.

"As false as Romeo's good nature!" he declared. "Well, if you really don't feel that you can come, I'll go. Have a good time in Dublin," he added, stood up, waved a hand, and re-joined the fat woman, who had already started eating and had not once looked round at her 'son'.

Was this man Chloe's brother? Or was he creating confusion for the sake of it?

Rollison paid his bill and went to the lounge steps. Rumble waved, Rollison walked across the lounge, frowning. If he did telephone Scotland Yard, Grice might be able to get the Irish police to act promptly, but there was much in what Rumble had said; if he were an Irish citizen he might get some protection here. A tussle with the Irish police was the last thing Rollison wanted.

He stood at the top of the steps looking into Dawson Street as trains clattered by. There was reason for disquiet despite the tranquillity of the city just here. When had Rumble recognised him? When he had come into the dining-room, perhaps – but it was possible that he had been seen before and that Rumble had come with the deliberate purpose of accosting him. Was Rumble alone? Or did others work for him? Was there danger as he stood there – the danger that he had invited by keeping up Majors' shares, by taking any part in this affair? Would a bullet come out of the darkness of the turning opposite him – or out of the brightness of a neon sign which surrounded a shop window and doorway?

"*Penny, sir.*" It was a whispered voice, close beside him. He had not noticed a barefooted boy walk up by the railings and then sidle towards him. His face was dirty, his eyes sorrowful. "*Penny, sir,*" he whispered.

Rollison put his hand to his pocket.

"I shouldn't, if I were ye," declared a man who appeared from the street. He was beaming; he was beardless; but his voice was deep, like Rumble's – remarkably like it, in fact.

Rollison glanced behind him. Rumble and the woman were in the lounge.

"Send the little beggar away with a flea in his ear," advised the beardless man.

He grinned cheekily, and walked on.

Rollison stared after him. That encounter had been deliberately made, to confuse him. Two Rumbles – oh, there could be any number of men with rumbling voices. As he pondered, he began to smile; one could admire the cleverness of this attempt to spread confusion.

He heard a man whistling a tune beloved of Snub, a recent addition to Snub's repertoire. This man came into the light He was about Snub's build; he had a large moustache and his hair was cut rather short; but it was Snub who came up the steps, still whistling, and said, "Goodevening to ye," and walked into the hotel. Rollison did not follow immediately, but when he went inside he found Snub sitting in a dim corner. There were few seats available, but one was near Snub. Rollison wandered about aimlessly, and then took it.

Snub was reading an *Evening Mail*.

"You're being watched," he whispered.

"I know Rumble," said Rollison. "Why pick him out?"

"He was at Chelsea. I followed, leaving Peter and Alice inside. I know what happened from the papers. How's Alice?"

"All right," said Rollison.

"Anything I can do?" asked Snub.

"I'm going to watch for O'Brien at the post office, who will collect a round blue packet."

"Yes."

"That's a job for you, now that I'm watched."

"Thanks!"

"Who else is about?"

"Hilary—but I expect you know that. I don't know the others. Better not talk too much."

"Where shall I meet you?"

"Phoenix Park, shall we say?"

"It's a bit far out," whispered Rollison.

"O'Connell Bridge, then. This side." Snub had put his paper down and was looking about him. No one could have told that he was talking. Suddenly his eyes lit up, he jumped from his chair and, without another word, hurried across the lounge to a girl who had just come in. She was young and slender and pretty, and her eyes lit up in turn. Snub greeted her warmly, looking as if he would like to kiss her, and led her out almost immediately.

"Well, well!" exclaimed Rollison; and again he thought of Alice.

Snub had not even said where he was staying!

A page-boy came from a passage on the left, calling a name which Rollison did not recognise at first. "Mr. Rawlson, Mr. Rawlson, Mr. Rawlson, please!" He meant Rollison! Rollison raised a hand and the boy hurried towards him.

"There's a ca' from London for ye, sor."

"Thanks," said Rollison. "Where can I take it?"

"This way, please."

Rollison was led past the telephone exchange. There were three boxes, and from one of them a man, who seemed to be talking in a normal voice, could be clearly heard.

"I'll take it in my room," said Rollison, and hurried up the stairs. He crossed the room and lifted the receiver.

"Hallo."

"Good evening, sir," said Jolly, as if he were on the other side of the room. "I hope you have found your hotel comfortable."

"It's first class," said Rollison, "and S. is all right. You might tell Miss Hellier that."

"I will advise Lady Gloria," promised Jolly. "I am very glad to hear it, sir. I thought you would like to know that Mr. Hilary attempted to catch the night plane to Dublin—"

"He caught it."

"Without causing you any inconvenience, I hope," said Jolly. He was speaking very slowly and distinctly, and Rollison could not escape a feeling that there was something more on his mind. "I thought it wise to follow him. He visited Mr. Romeo at *Greengates* and I heard some part of the conversation. Romeo gave him instructions to try to catch the plane. There was nothing at all furtive, the police were also within earshot. Hilary's instructions are to try to find who is buying Majors' shares in Dublin."

"I see," said Rollison.

"There is one other thing …" Jolly began, and paused.

"Yes."

"Miss Hellier left the Marigold Club with Lady Gloria late this evening, and was parted from her in the crowd in Piccadilly. Lady Gloria is somewhat perturbed. I am keeping in constant touch with her in the hope that Miss Hellier returns to the club or comes here. I am sorry that the news is so vague, sir."

Rollison said, slowly: "Well, I suppose that can't be helped. Is there anything else?"

"Nothing, sir. Good night," said Jolly.

"Good night," echoed Rollison.

The news that Alice was no longer in Aunt Gloria's charge oppressed him. He had never really satisfied himself that she had told him the whole truth. He recalled that night drive and the sound from behind him, the dark head bobbing up, the shyness of her approach contrasting so oddly with the resourcefulness of her action. Calvert had tried to kill her and it was now certain that Calvert did not work on his own.

Was she safe?

Surely the police had watched her with redoubled care after the death of the man who had been following Peter. Grice's men might slip up once but the Yard would be on its mettle after that.

The telephone bell broke across his thoughts.

He looked at it for some seconds, then leaned forward and lifted it. He expected to hear Rumble's deep voice. Instead, he heard Snub's.

"I'm sorry I dashed off like that," said Snub, in a low-pitched voice. "I had a feeling that we were being watched, and as I'd made a date—"

"You haven't much time to waste on dates," said Rollison.

"My dear boss, no! But a little local colour is always useful. I've told her I'm a reporter and liable to be rushed off at a moment's notice. Nice eyes, hasn't she?"

"Very," said Rollison. "Where are you staying?"

"Round the corner, at the Gresham."

"In what name?"

"Higgs."

"All right. Don't use the telephone too much. Remember we're looking for Calvert as well as keeping an eye open for Hilary, Rumble and, possibly, Alice Hellier."

"*What?*"

"I'll be somewhere near the post office tomorrow morning," Rollison told him, "and later at the bridge. Anything else?"

"Not yet," said Snub, heavily. "If anything happens to *that* girl—" He broke off, but there was no doubt that the news stung him.

"Don't be surprised if you can't find me here after tonight," said Rollison.

He rang off, got up and went to the door. A man was walking along the passage, but there was nothing to indicate that he had been standing by the door. He went downstairs, and Rollison saw his face clearly; he was plump and red, and Rollison thought that he was Irish.

Rollison went back and closed the door.

The affair oppressed him too often. There was too great a measure of uncertainty. He kept seeing Alice Hellier's face in his mind's eye, and the mood of uncertainty possessed him for the next half an hour, while he packed everything he had taken out of his case except a square tin – a theatrical make-up box which Jolly had thoughtfully put in. He went out with that in his hand.

He was watched as he crossed the crowded lounge; but then most of the people present were idling and looking at the passers-by. He went out and turned left, then left again into Graham Street. He idled outside Trinity College and, when a crowd had collected beside the traffic policeman, he slipped across the road. He walked swiftly, glancing behind him occasionally, but saw no indication that he was being followed. The trouble was that if Rumble took off that beard he would not be recognisable. Who was Rumble? Could his statement that he was Chloe Romeo's brother be accepted? It was not even possible to be sure that the woman he had been with was the girl's mother, or his own.

On the far side of the bridge in O'Connell Street he felt confident that he had not been followed. He took a side street and a little way along saw an illuminated hotel sign. He went into a narrow entrance and stood there for some minutes. No one showed any interest in him.

The reception office of the hotel was on the first floor and a sleepy-looking porter looked up in vague inquiry at the stranger.

Rollison beamed at him.

"*Good* evening. Have you a room by any chance?"

"Well, now, we have—"

"Splendid!" said Rollison, and took out his wallet. Payment in advance satisfied the porter; so did the name of Ross.

Soon he was in a small, poorly furnished room in which a dim light burned over the dressing-table which had a single mirror. He locked the door, opened the make-up box and selected one of several moustaches; he fastened it to his upper lip with spirit gum, and then used greasepaint to darken the skin under his eyes and to put lines about his mouth. He worked intently for twenty minutes, and when he had finished leaned back and surveyed his reflection.

It was reasonable, but it would not pass a close inspection. His clothes would give him away to anyone who knew him fairly well. He had thought himself prepared, but needed many more things. He knew no one in Dublin from whom he could borrow, and there was no point in buying a different outfit next morning – unless he went to a second-hand shop for a suit which just about fitted.

He went to bed, still oppressed. Snub was back, but Alice had gone.

The sun shone brightly through his window next morning, and a good breakfast of Irish bacon and eggs put new life into him. He left the hotel before nine o'clock. A different porter was on duty and so his changed appearance was not noticed.

He went towards Queensbridge Station, but on the north side of the river. Not far along, down a side street, he entered a second-hand clothes shop; soon he was out with a parcel under his arm. He changed at the small hotel, left his own clothes parcelled up to be called for, and made his way to the main post office.

Snub was already on duty.

Rollison walked past the youngster, who did not give him a second glance. That cheered Rollison. He looked about him, hoping to find a café where he could sit and watch, but none was open. He stood in the doorway of a shop for a while, wondering what time the London mail arrived; it was possible that the morning's vigil would be wasted.

People crowded into the post office while Snub sauntered up and down, doing a creditable job of looking disinterested in anyone. He watched those who came out more closely than those who went in.

A barefooted street arab approached Snub with newspapers, and while Snub's attention was distracted, a man came out of the post office putting a rolled parcel inside his pocket. It was packed in blue paper, as Grice had promised, and was about the size of a roll which Rollison had taken from Calvert's desk.

Snub pushed a coin into the boy's hand, then saw the man with the roll.

A man bearded, and like Rumble, followed him.

The man with the roll was short, square-shouldered and jaunty. He had fair hair, curly at the sides, and was a little splay-footed. He seemed not to have a care in the world as he walked towards O'Connell Bridge. Snub was no more than ten yards behind him, Rollison twenty yards farther behind, the bearded man at a safe distance. *Was* that Rumble?

Rollison saw a car slowing down alongside Snub but gave it little thought until it passed him and stopped by the fair-haired man. He checked the cry of warning which came to his lips, and saw Snub glance round, as if hoping to see a taxi.

A man inside the car leaned out, snatched the roll from the fair-haired man, leaving him gaping on the pavement, while the car moved off at high speed. Snub let out a bellow, to attract attention, but the car was already some way off. It swung right over the bridge, squeezing past a green tram. Snub was running fast as Rollison saw the passenger of the car leaning out of the window – he had a spade-shaped beard.

The bearded pedestrian boarded a tram going in the opposite direction.

Two men who looked like Rumble were in Dublin; and undoubtedly the second was there only to confuse Rollison.

But that was not important at the moment.

Rollison reached the fair-haired messenger's side. This must be O'Brien – his first charge now.

The man was still gaping after the disappearing car, and in his eyes there was such a look of chagrin that Rollison had it in his heart to be sorry for him; but not to let him go.

"Mr. O'Brien, I believe," he said.

O'Brien started and swung round.

"Who—"

"I want you," said Rollison.

"I—"

"I shouldn't make a fuss," warned Rollison.

He thought O'Brien was going to make a dash for safety, but the man suddenly dropped his arms in resignation; the fight went out of him. It happened suspiciously quickly, a fact which Rollison did not fail to notice.

"You'd better come with me," said Rollison, and, taking his arm as any policeman would, led him along by the river.

Chapter Nineteen

The Frightened Man

O'Brien seemed to have lost his nerve completely. He did not shake Rollison's hand away, and walked meekly alongside him. Rollison was trying to decide how best to tackle him; while he was in this state he would probably talk freely. As they walked, the clip-clop-clip-clop of a horse's hooves sounded behind them. Rollison turned, to see a hansom cab with its old bowler-hatted driver slouching in his seat.

Rollison called, "Are you engaged?"

"No, sor. Whoa, there, Biddy!"

"What—" began O'Brien.

"Get inside," said Rollison. He opened the door and bundled the man in, then called: "Phoenix Park." That meant a fairly long drive, and once in the park they could drive for miles without interference. The horse started off at a good clipping pace, while Rollison and O'Brien sat side by side, the Irishman confused and bewildered.

"Who are ye?" demanded O'Brien, hoarsely.

A notion flashed into Rollison's mind.

"I'm from Romeo," he said.

"Romeo!" gasped O'Brien. "Rom—" He broke off, and licked his lips. Now he was really frightened. The hansom rattled and swayed over a stretch of cobbled road; their knees kept touching, traffic and people surged about them; yet inside the cab it seemed quiet,

"What—what do you want?" asked O'Brien.

"Calvert."

"He—I—" The Irishman broke off and turned and looked out of the window. So he knew where Calvert was; presumably he had come from Calvert that morning. It would have been better, thought Rollison, to have followed the man to his destination. He changed his mind; Calvert would not be so easily frightened and would be less likely to talk.

"It isn't my fault at all!" gasped O'Brien, leaning forward and grasping Rollison's arm. "I tell ye, it isn't any fault of me own. I've been made to do it. I—"

And the story bubbled out of him as the cab lurched on.

There were so many things in Ireland that were hard to obtain in England, especially in the two years after the war, said O'Brien, wasn't it natural that a man who often travelled to England should smuggle a little out when he could? Och, it was not a crime! There wasn't a cleaner living man in all Ireland, but a few trifles …

The trifles had been jewels and furs. He had sold them to Calvert, who at the time had been manager of a provincial departmental store. The smuggling had increased as greed increased, and soon O'Brien had found himself a helpless tool in the hands of Calvert and others, some of whom he could not name. Had he tried to rebel his past sins would have been brought against him, and O'Brien had found himself in the cleft stick of blackmail; it did not seem to Rollison that the man would have been greatly troubled had there been no fear of being found out. Gone was his jauntiness and confidence, and his manner was a measure of his fear.

Recently the smuggled goods had been going to Majors.

"Through Calvert?" asked Rollison.

"Och, and who else?" But they had been sent to a man named Lund, a Peter Lund.

O'Brien was so obsessed with his own plight that he did not notice Rollison's expression then. He plunged on. Calvert had arrived in Ireland the previous day, with his story, demanding help – and getting it. He had telephoned some instructions to Hilary and today had sent O'Brien to collect a parcel; it was like the man to make him use his own name, declared O'Brien, angrily, but there had seemed no risk in it. Calvert had appeared to think that whatever he said Hilary would do what he was told – and hadn't he just?

When he had seen Rumble …

"Do you know Rumble?" asked Rollison, sharply.

"Och, yes, the man's always making a nuisance of himself," said O'Brien, wiping his face. He looked out of the window into the rolling parkland of Phoenix Park, and stared at the distant trees. "How much he knows or guesses I couldn't tell ye, sor, but it's more than enough for my peace of mind, that it is."

"Does Calvert know him?"

"I think they've met," said O'Brien cautiously.

"Where's Calvert now?"

O'Brien drew in a short breath.

"He's staying wid me, where else would he go?"

"And where is that?" asked Rollison.

For the first time O'Brien showed signs of obstinacy, but that quickly faded. He lived in a village on the borders of County Dublin, just beyond Dundrum; it was a fine home and the gentleman wouldn't be disappointed in it. Calvert was living there on the fat of the land and expecting him back at any time. Calvert often came to Ireland for a night, flying over on the evening or afternoon aircraft and returning on the first one next morning; that explained his absences from his Hendon rooms, and disposed of the idea that he lived a Jekyll and Hyde existence in England. Dundrum was too far to be reached with comfort in a hansom, said O'Brien – and what was the gentleman going to do with him? What – what did Romeo know about him?

Rollison knocked on the trap in the roof and told the driver to return to town, then sat down and lit a cigarette. O'Brien's blue eyes were starting from his head. He had lost nothing of his fear.

"Why are you frightened of Romeo?" demanded Rollison.

"Och, and who wouldn't be? Doesn't Romeo know that Calvert's been cheating him, and doesn't Rumble work for him?"

"Are you sure of that?"

"For whom else would he be working?" demanded O'Brien. "He's Romeo's brother-in-law."

"Where does Rumble live?" asked Rollison, omitting to remind O'Brien that he had said he knew nothing about Rumble.

"I wouldn't be knowing that," said O'Brien, "but it's a house in Black Rock where his mother lives. The sight of it!" Before his sister married Romeo they had a little shop in Rathgar, just a little shop, and the girl worked in a shop in Dublin itself before she went on the stage. And now they had a fine house in Black Rock, which was near Dun Laoghaire and on the sea, and they lived in luxury. "They?" queried Rollison. Chloe Romeo's mother and younger sisters; the husband had been killed in the troubles, years ago.

Yes, Rollison thought, it was quite possible that Rumble worked for Romeo, and that Romeo knew something of Calvert's activities, although the fat man had pretended to know nothing at all.

When they reached the city Rollison paid off the cabby, giving him a prodigious sum. Rollison expected O'Brien to try to get away, but he seemed quite numbed by what had happened, and stood meekly by. Yet now and again he shot Rollison a cunning glance, and Rollison wondered whether he had reasoned that if Rollison really came from Romeo, it was odd that he knew so little about the family in Dublin.

A streamlined American taxi drew near.

Rollison put up a hand and the taxi stopped. O'Brien stepped in without any argument and directed the driver to his village near Dundrum. They were driven with the speed and recklessness of a Paris taxi through the city and towards the countryside, passing little one-storeyed cottages, most of them freshly washed in white, and field after field where pigs abounded. They came to a high wall and, a little way past it, a collection of tiny houses and a small church. A priest was standing at the gate of a house and waved when he saw O'Brien.

O'Brien waved back. "Good-day' to ye, Father!"

"Is it visitors you're having today?"

"Me friends are always welcome," called O'Brien, as the taxi-driver turned into a drive between iron gates.

Immediately in front of them was an old Georgian house, a square and ugly building, standing gaunt and erect out of unkempt grounds. A dog came rushing towards them and then sniffed and squealed as O'Brien got out of the car. O'Brien spoke to it as if to a child, and the dog frisked.

"I won't be long," Rollison said to the driver.

O'Brien turned and looked at him with the cunning gleam in his eye. He was certainly no fool. Rollison walked with him to the front door. The taxi-driver was within call and the village was only just beyond the high wall, but Calvert was supposed to be here, and known to be desperate. Rollison wished that he had a weapon in his pocket, but he went on without looking back. He would risk much for an hour's talk with Calvert.

A slip of a girl in a blue overall opened the door.

"Hallo, Bridget, me pet," said O'Brien, and took Rollison's arm. "There isn't a better girl in all Ireland than Bridget, Mister, that you can take for a fact."

Bridget simpered and hurried over rich carpets towards a door which led to the right. The hall was well furnished; there was money here, more money than a man like O'Brien might be expected to have. They went into a vast sitting-room where a red setter rose from a spot near the window and stood watching carelessly, wagging his great tail.

"There isn't a finer specimen in all Ireland," boasted O'Brien.

He was not thinking about what he was saying. He was more jaunty, now, as if he had reason to be pleased with himself. Doubtless he had not expected to lure Rollison here alone, and he was planning a trick. He would turn the tables as soon as he thought himself safe; and perhaps he thought he was safe already.

He led the way along a narrow stone passage beyond the sitting-room. It struck cold. At the end was a narrow wooden door, and he stood with his fingers on the handle and lowered his voice.

"Ye understand that Calvert isn't known to be here, sor; he lives downstairs and I look after him myself; it wouldn't do for Bridget to know, she gossips so much. He's quite comfortable down here, he'll be asleep no doubt."

"At this hour?"

"We were awake half the night," said O'Brien, and gave a wide yawn. "It's hard to keep awake this morning at all." He opened the door and stood aside. "I'll follow ye," he added.

"You lead the way," said Rollison.

"Och, if you wish it, I will."

There was a cupboard containing a few old coats and, in the wall, another door which O'Brien opened and which led to a flight of steps.

It was dark below. Rollison could hear no sound. He looked into O'Brien's eyes and saw the glitter of triumph; yes, O'Brien thought that he had been clever, and down here he would try to render him useless; he had no cause to congratulate himself.

He switched on a light. A dim glow spread about the narrow wooden staircase and the blank space below. He went down noisily, whistling as if to keep his spirits up, but undoubtedly intending to warn Calvert or whoever *was* here …

Rollison found himself a prey to doubts and fears, as he walked steadily down the stairs. O'Brien reached the bottom where there were two doors, one closed, the other ajar.

"Calvert!" called O'Brien, "I've brought—"

The door which was ajar moved slowly. Rollison stood behind O'Brien, watching close, ready to attack if there seemed danger, trying to see the reason for O'Brien's behaviour. He saw a hand at the door – and the hand moved upwards, something swung through the air.

"*Begorrah!*" screamed O'Brien,

The missile hit the electric bulb and plunged them into darkness. Rollison was near the stairs, and tensed himself to withstand an attack, O'Brien was as alarmed and surprised as he.

A powerful beam shot out from a torch.

"*Begorrah!*" sighed O'Brien.

A shot rang oat.

The flash of the flame was weak against the beam of the torch, which was shining on O'Brien's face. O'Brien did not cry but threw up his hand – and the beam swept round towards Rollison, who closed his eyes and leapt towards it, striking at the hand which held it. He touched the torch. He heard a gasp; the torch clattered to the stone floor. A man bumped into him and he heard the sough of breath as his fist landed into the unknown's stomach. Then a hand caught him on the side of the head and swept him to one side. The torch was out, blackness enveloped them. He heard footsteps on the stairs, the man had passed him and was rushing up. Rollison turned and stumbled in his wake, but the man had a good lead.

Was it Calvert?

The door at the head of the stairs opened and a glimmer of light shone through. Rollison saw a bearded man standing for a second at the head of the stairs with a gun in his hand.

"I'll wish ye good-bye!" cried Rumble.

He spoke with a broad Irish accent he had never revealed before, and there was a laughing note in his voice. He slammed the door. Rollison stood half-way up the stairs, feeling a surge of relief because he had not been hurt; and then he hurried up to the door.

He pushed it, but nothing happened; it was locked on the outside. He stood for a long time close to the door, hearing no sound, conscious only of the darkness, remembering the cry and then the sigh which had come from O'Brien.

The torch might not be broken.

Touching the wall, he felt his way down the stairs and lit his lighter when he reached the foot. The little flame shone upon O'Brien, who lay in a crumpled heap; and that reminded him of Peter lying dead on a carpet of duck-egg blue. He saw the torch, picked it up and flashed it on.

He put the torch on the floor, where it shone on O'Brien's head and shoulders; then he knelt beside the man and felt his pulse. That was mere formality, for O'Brien had been shot through the head.

He let the limp hand fall.

There was still no sound, and outside the taxi-driver was waiting, and doubtless the priest was talking to his flock or walking along a country road. And Rumble …

Who *was* Rumble? *Which* Rumble?

As the man had called out in that rollicking voice there had seemed to Rollison something familiar about him, something which he knew and could not place.

He put the questions out of his mind.

He had not yet grappled with his own plight; he wanted to know what else he would find here. He picked up the torch and went through the open doorway into a room which was small but, as far as he could see, well furnished. There was a carpet on the floor, an easy chair and, picked out by the bright light, a row of bottles and glasses on a trolley near the wall. The mask of a woman's head, a futuristic, hideous thing, seemed to glare at him. He swung the torch round; the light fell upon the body of a man.

Calvert had been dead a few minutes longer than O'Brien. He, too, had been shot at close quarters, but in the chest.

So the man was twice a murderer.

The air of the cellars struck cold. Rollison switched on a light and the room seemed to get smaller. It was luxurious in its fashion, and tobacco smoke hung over it in a grey haze. He did not look at Calvert again, except to see that the man's coat was flung open; Rumble had been through his pockets.

He looked on the table.

There were the drawings, each one separate, spread about as if each had been closely inspected. Rollison picked one up by the edges, anxious not to blur fingerprints which Rumble might have made. He still pushed away the thought of his own plight. The pictures looked identical with those which he had found, and he counted them – there were eight sheets. So Rumble had examined them and pushed them aside, presumably considering them useless – unless he had read their message, and that was all he had wanted to do.

Rollison took out a handkerchief, rolled the papers up in it, and then rolled the blue wrapping paper about it.

He searched the room, but found nothing of interest.

He stepped over Calvert's body and, in the hall, over O'Brien's. The house seemed as silent as the death which it harboured. He tried the handle of the other door, and it opened. He groped for a light switch, pressed it down, and found himself on the threshold of a store-room. There were crates piled to the ceiling against the walls in places, and some steel cabinets and a big safe. The safe was locked. Rollison went to one of the packing-cases and saw that it had been wrenched open. He lifted the lid and, standing on tiptoe, peered inside. The lovely, dark smoothness of mink lay there. He pulled another case towards him and lifted out a coat – in England it would be worth several thousand pounds. There were four other coats in that box.

He stood back, and read the black lettering on the outside: *'Pure Irish Linen.'*

He went out and bent over O'Brien, whom Rumble could not have searched; and he found keys in the man's hip pockets. One of them was for a Random safe; and the safe in the corner was a Random.

The key fitted.

Rollison pulled at the heavy door. He had to exert all his strength to get it open, and found himself looking at a dozen jewel cases, each with a small padlock. Using a handkerchief to avoid leaving prints, he took one case beneath the light, glanced round and found a small cold chisel and a claw-headed hammer, and prised the case open.

Jewels flashed and sparkled, all stones of incalculable worth.

"Well, well!" breathed Rollison.

He put the case back in the safe, closed the door, locked it and then stood back, breathing hard, coming face to face now with the fact that he was locked in a cellar with two dead men, and that he knew only one way out. He examined the walls; they offered no means of escape. Nor did the other room or the bathroom which led from it.

What he needed most was to call the Civic Guards.

He smiled ironically and went up the stairs. Light from both rooms shone to the top, and he did not need to use the torch. He examined the lock of the door closely, and pulled a face; it was another Random and there was no chance of opening it from the inside, little chance from the outside except with a key. He lit a cigarette and stood listening intently. He heard nothing. He tapped on the door, which looked like wood but was of steel. He knew how carefully that cellar had been sealed off, now …

Would one of O'Brien's keys open the door?

Curiously enough, it hadn't been locked, O'Brien had just pulled it open.

He began to try the keys. He was intent on the task when something moved – a slight movement, hardly enough to attract his attention. It was the handle, which was being turned from the outside.

Chapter Twenty

Council Of Three

Rollison turned and went down the stairs, peering over his shoulder to see whether the door opened, but he reached the foot of the stairs before it did. He stood in the doorway of the lounge, listening intently.

He heard the door open.

No one spoke, but there were footsteps, cautious and slow. He stayed in his hiding-place. He thought he heard a man catch his breath, perhaps at the sight of O'Brien's body. Rollison backed farther into the lounge and half-closed the door. He could see O'Brien from a gap near the hinges. The footsteps drew nearer and soon he saw the shadow of a man cast on the opposite wall.

The man came into sight, looking down at O'Brien.

It was Hilary!

Hilary looked very young as he stood staring down and then, moving slowly and as if horrified, stretched out a hand to touch the dead man. He did not flinch when his fingers touched O'Brien's cheeks, but he bent down and felt his heart and his pulse. Then he straightened up and looked helplessly about him.

He said slowly: "There won't be a doctor in this one-eyed hole."

He turned and hurried upstairs.

He behaved as if he had no idea that he was being watched, reached the top of the stairs and hurried across the wooden floor. Rollison went quickly after him. Freedom was at hand, but he was interested only in Hilary. The youngster did not call out to the maid, but went through the lounge to the hall.

He lifted a telephone, and Rollison heard him say: "Put me through to a doctor—"

"Try the Civic Guards," advised Rollison.

He moved into sight and Hilary almost dropped the telephone. He caught at it, saved it from falling, and stood with it by his side. The operator was saying something; her voice, although not her words, echoed about the hall.

"Who …" began Hilary, and stopped.

"I'm not a ghost."

"Rollison!"

"A tribute to the disguise, anyhow," said Rollison. He took the telephone from Hilary's grasp; the girl at the exchange was saying patiently: "Will you speak to me? Is it a doctor you want?"

"I would like to speak to the Civic Guard barracks nearest Dundrum," said Rollison.

"Then ye won't have to go far from Dundrum," said the girl; "if ye'll hold on a moment I'll put ye through."

Hilary was still staring.

"It—it's uncanny!" he gasped. "I wouldn't have recognised you but for the voice. Those—those clothes!"

"Now we know what makes the man," said Rollison. "The police will be here pretty soon, and you'll have to explain what you were doing."

"Explain—"

"Now get a hold on yourself!" exclaimed Rollison. "You were going to send for a doctor, weren't you? You were going to let it be known that you were here."

"I—well, yes," said Hilary. "I—seeing that man dead down there upset me. I followed Rumble here earlier, lost him in the grounds, and saw him clearing off a few minutes ago. I got in—"

Rollison said: "And went straight to the cellar door, unlocked it and came downstairs. A likely story."

Hilary said, "Well, it—it's partly true."

Rollison touched his shoulder.

"The Irish police aren't any more foolish than ours," he said, "and you'll have to have something better than that for them. What were you doing here?"

"If it comes to that," retorted Hilary, "what are you doing here? And that man—Rollison!" He backed away. "Did—did you—*kill* him?"

"I just led him to his death," said Rollison, with a touch of bitterness. "You say you followed … Hallo!" A deep voice sounded on the telephone. "Civic Guard … I am speaking from the home of Mr. O'Brien, near Dundrum … Yes, that's the house … Mr. O'Brien has met with a serious accident … Yes, at once, please."

The man at the other end did not waste time.

Rollison replaced the receiver, took out cigarettes and handed the case to Hilary. The youngster took one with fingers which were a trifle unsteady. There was no other sound in the big house, but birds were flashing across the garden, chattering shrilly, and outside a bus rumbled by, in sight one moment, then lost behind the high wall.

The taxi had gone.

"How did Rumble leave?" asked Rollison.

"There was a taxi outside …"

Rollison shrugged. "Well, we'll have to walk. You don't want to be questioned, do you?"

"I—no, I suppose I don't."

"And I most certainly don't," said Rollison. "Pull your hat well over your eyes and let's get out."

Rollison was not likely to be recognised. If Hilary had been deceived, the disguise was more effective than he had realised. Vague thoughts were running through his mind; the most important that he must talk to Hilary and find out how he had come across Rumble and what he was doing here – how, for instance, had he found that door?

Hilary pulled his hat low over his eyes.

No one appeared to notice them. They went down the steps at the front of the house, then round to the back. A girl was singing in a loud voice. She was standing at a sink, sideways towards them, and the soft turf muffled the sound of their footsteps. They reached a hedge at the back of the house and, as they passed through a gap in it, they saw an old man working in the garden. He was bending over and did not see them, but when Rollison glanced over his shoulder he saw the old man look up and gaze speculatively towards them.

"Stay out of sight." said Rollison to Hilary.

Then he went to the gardener and asked: "Have you seen a man with a beard nearby?"

"I have an' all," said the gardener, in a creaky voice.

"Where did he go?" asked Rollison.

"Now would I be knowing? I was at the front of the house, now, and he went off in a car. The Devil must ha' been chasing him, he was in such a hurry."

Then he went on with his work.

Rollison rejoined Hilary and they went to the far end of the hedge, where they climbed a wire fence. Ploughed fields spread before them. They kept near the hedge and headed for the main road. There was little traffic, and Rollison began to wonder how they would get back to Dublin; it was six or seven miles from here and he had no desire to walk. Too many people would notice two city-dressed strangers walking, in any case.

A car passed them as they reached the road; the driver was in blue uniform.

"There go the police," remarked Rollison.

"Didn't—didn't you ask for the Civic Guard?"

"It's the same thing here," said Rollison. "Don't you know Ireland well enough for that?"

"I don't know it and I don't want to know it," Hilary said feelingly. "The sooner I'm out of the country the better I'll like it. If Romeo knew everything—"

"But you came on his instructions."

"I work for him," retorted Hilary. "And I believe in him!"

"I see," said Rollison.

Hilary was anxious to talk.

"Look here, I can't help it if the man I work for gives me instructions I don't understand," he said defensively. "He told me to come over here, keep an eye open for Rumble and come to this place before I went back, and see a fellow named O'Brien. He told me about the door along that passage. Damn it," exploded Hilary, "he gave me a key!"

"Did he, by George!"

"And here it is," declared Hilary, snatching a key from his pocket. "What on earth is Romeo up to?"

"Well, you've obeyed instructions."

"I haven't seen O'Brien."

"You have," said Rollison.

"That—dead man?"

Rollison nodded. Hilary tightened his lips, but did not speak. They came across a signpost on which was written in characteristic Irish lettering: '*bus*'. There was no timetable, but a solitary cyclist was making his way towards them and Rollison beckoned him. The man went out of his way to be helpful; there would be a bus in about ten minutes' time, there was one every half-hour. Yes, it would take them to the centre of Dublin, they had only to take their seats and keep them. He went off, saying that it was a fine hard day, and wobbled out of sight.

They said little until the bus arrived on time; twenty minutes later they were getting out near the Gresham Hotel. They walked in silence towards it, and then Hilary asked: "Where are you staying?"

"In Dublin," said Rollison, laconically.

"Oh, don't be a fool! Great Scott do I want a drink!" Hilary led the way into the Gresham Hotel, and a waiter came to them at once. Hilary took off his hat and dropped it on to a chair; soon he was tossing down a whisky and soda. He lit a cigarette and stared about him, and at last looked straight at the Toff.

"We'd better talk in my room, hadn't we?"

"All right," said Rollison, deliberately letting him have his head.

The big house at Dundrum seemed to fade from his memory. The events of the morning had become vague. He was anxious to get rid of his disguise but more anxious to talk to Hilary, who looked at breaking point.

The room was large and comfortable. Hilary flung himself down on the bed and motioned Rollison to a chair.

"How long have you been here?" he demanded.

"We were on the same plane," said Rollison.

"I—Good lord! And I didn't see you!" Rollison made no comment. Hilary brushed his hair back and went on: "Look here, Rollison, I don't know what you're up to, but I do know you were shut in with a dead man, and—"

"Blame Rumble."

"Rumble!"

"What do you know about him?" asked Rollison.

Then Hilary's story bubbled out of him, much as O'Brien's had done. Rollison knew everything up to the time that Hilary had left London – he knew about the murder of Peter Lund and the stock position and all that kind of thing. Well, the previous afternoon Romeo had sent for him to visit Greengates and told him to come to Dublin and look for Rumble and O'Brien. He described his brother-in-law as a man with a beard which no one could miss – yes, Romeo seemed to think that it was a natural beard. How Romeo knew about O'Brien and O'Brien's house Hilary did not know. Romeo had told him that he thought O'Brien might be able to tell him where to find Calvert. He, Romeo, had given Hilary five thousand pounds *in cash*, with which to bribe O'Brien into giving Calvert away. If Hilary found Calvert, he was to show no sign and telephone Romeo, who would take the necessary action.

"I think he meant to fly over here," said Hilary. "He thinks he can deal with Calvert if he finds him. I'll tell you one thing, Rollison, this is a murky business *and* Romeo's involved more deeply than we realise."

"Probably," conceded Rollison. "And you found Rumble."

"He's staying here in this hotel. I followed him this morning."

"How?"

"By taxi. I paid the man off, I didn't know when I'd want him again. And Rumble shook me off in the grounds. I went to a cottage half a mile behind the house, thinking I'd seen him, but it was empty. Romeo had described the house pretty clearly; I felt sure it was O'Brien's. The front door wasn't locked, and I went to the door that Romeo had told me about. You—you know what happened then."

"I see," said Rollison.

Hilary sat up. "Now what about *you*?"

Rollison told him of the encounter with O'Brien and the theft of the papers and Rumble's apparent lack of interest in them. But as he talked he realised that it was impossible to prove that the man at the house had been Rumble. It had been someone with a spade-shaped beard and a voice which sounded like the mystery man's; that was no evidence for a court of law. He dwelt for a moment on the legal side of this situation; the Civic Guards would set up a hue-and-cry for the murderers, his description and Hilary's *might* be broadcast; it was as important to get Hilary back to England as to get back himself.

Hilary threw up his hands.

"Well, it beats me!"

"What time's the next plane to London?" asked Rollison.

"Twelve-thirty, I think,"

Rollison looked at his watch. "You've just time to catch it," he said. "They can't have a description of you put out just yet. Get back, tell Romeo exactly what happened and tell him I'll see him tomorrow. And you might try to find out what those drawings mean," he added.

"Drawings?" queried Hilary.

So apparently he knew nothing about them. Rollison explained a little and Hilary shrugged his shoulders. He protested against catching the 12.30 plane; there would be little time. He was anxious enough to get back to England, but …

There was a tap at the door.

Hilary started and then jumped from the bed. Rollison stepped swiftly to the door and stood behind it, then signed to Hilary to tell the caller to come in. Hilary's voice was unsteady when he obeyed.

The door opened at once and Snub walked in.

Snub pushed the door to behind him and stared at Hilary and then about the room, his lips parted. "I could have sworn that Rollison was here," he said, and then turned and looked at Rollison.

Suddenly he beamed.

"Hallo, Chief!"

"What are you doing here?" demanded Hilary, roughly.

"I thought there might be room for me in the council," said Snub, cheerfully. "Three heads are better than two, in the circumstances." He glanced at Rollison's feet and widened his eyes. "Been farming?" he asked.

Rollison chuckled.

"I've been following O'Brien."

Snub pulled a face.

"I thought I saw you with him. Don't blame me too much," he pleaded, not greatly worried about being censured. "Rumble pulled one and that's that, I'm afraid. Any confession from O'Brien?"

"Nothing much," said Rollison.

Hilary looked at him sharply.

"What do you mean, nothing much? If he was dead when you found him—"

Snub whistled. *More* murder!"

"More murder and a lot of other things," said Rollison. "I told you that I'd led him there," he went on to Hilary; "he was shot while standing by my side."

"Rumble?" asked Snub, quietly.

"Yes."

"Bright boy, Rumble. I've just seen him."

Hilary snapped. "Where?"

"At a house in a suburb called Black Rock, I think," said Snub. "I spotted him while I was hanging about here, hoping that you'd turn up, Hilary. He looked in and then went out again, took a cab to this house, and sent the cab off. I couldn't make up my mind what to do," he added, for Rollison's benefit. "I placed the house and learned from neighbours that it's owned by a Mrs. Higgis, and Miss Higgis is ..." He paused, hoping to cause a sensation.

"We know who Chloe Higgis is," said Hilary, impatiently.

Snub concealed his disappointment.

"Oh well! I fancied I'd do more good about here, Chief. I thought you'd try to contact me here, and I was downstairs when you came in. Behind an *Irish Times*. Well, what's the next step?"

"Hilary's going back to report to Romeo," said Rollison.

"I'll never catch the twelve-thirty *now*," declared Hilary.

"There's another plane at half past two," Snub said, "and I've reserved a seat in case there was need to rush back. You can take it." He was playing up to Rollison, restraining his curiosity well, "Then what?" he asked.

"We'll probably go back this evening," said Rollison.

He was surprised that Hilary did not raise any further protest. The youngster seemed only too eager to get out of Ireland, and it may have been because of the memory of the dead body and the knowledge that he might have been seen and recognised. He started to pack, agreed to meet the others in the lounge, and Rollison and Snub went downstairs.

"Well?" asked Snub, hopefully.

"It's moving, and Calvert's dead. More Rumble. If Hilary's told the truth and got his facts right, the pointing finger is at Romeo."

"Would that surprise you?"

"No," admitted Rollison, as they sat down. He ordered drinks, and then added: "Now I've got to get rid of this greasepaint and get into some different clothes. Have you got anything else?"

"No."

"See Hilary on to the plane and then telephone me at the Hibernian," said Rollison. "It doesn't matter if Rumble spots me now."

"Pressure off?" remarked Snub.

"I think most of the Irish end is closed up," said Rollison. "Smuggling of furs and jewels on a pretty big scale, with Majors involved." He stood up. "The police will be after two strangers seen near the house where O'Brien was killed, that's why I want Hilary out of the country in a hurry."

"Ho-ho! You've certainly got to get that greasepaint off," said Snub. "It's not bad. Er—talking of disguises."

"Yes?"

"That Rumble beard," mused Snub, eyeing Rollison keenly. "Put one like it on any dark, curly-haired man and you wouldn't be able to tell the difference. Elementary, I know, and you've spotted it, but it's worth mentioning. I mean, how many Rumbles? The merchant doesn't mind showing himself, and if he has one or two stooges about, he could fake an alibi anywhere. Had you thought of it?"

"I haven't thought enough about it," said Rollison. He finished his drink. "Don't forget to see Hilary off," he added, "and I'll see you at the Hibernian about four."

"Okay, chief! Er ..." Snub's expression changed ... "No news of Alice?"

"I'm afraid not," said Rollison.

Snub looked sombre when he left the hotel. He went to the smaller one, collected his clothes and changed and took off his make-up before he went back to the Hibernian.

It was after four when Snub sent a message to Rollison's room at the Hibernian, saying he had arrived. Rollison, dressed in his own clothes and himself again, hurried downstairs. Snub was standing near the post-box in the main entrance, looking at an *Evening Mail*. He glanced up, his eyes glowing.

"You've got nearly all the front page," he said. "Two bodies—was the other Calvert's?"

"Yes. Let's get out to Black Rock," said Rollison. "I want a talk with Chloe's mother."

"With what in mind?"

"The general situation," said Rollison. "I've a feeling that Rumble might be there."

Rumble was not there.

A removal van was standing outside the house, and the foreman in charge was garrulous. His men stood round and listened as he talked for the sake of hearing himself talk. Gradually, Rollison learned that the furniture was going into store, that the ladies who lived at the house were moving south – and that the removal firm had been paid in cash for the work.

As they moved away, Snub broke a long miserable silence.

"Now I know I should have stayed here," he said. "Birds flown—and Rumble. I wish we knew where to find Alice."

Rollison said slowly: "Does Alice matter like that?"

Snub shrugged and forced a smile.

"Yes. Odd, isn't it. I hardly know her, but don't rub it in." He drew a deep breath and smiled more freely. "Let's change the subject. Show your infallibility by telling me Rumble's real name."

Rollison raised his eyebrows.

"Your guess is as good as mine," he said. "We ought to phone Grice."

Chapter Twenty-One

Recall

Snub was thoughtful and smoked in silence on the way back to the Hibernian. Both of them bought a paper as soon as they reached the hotel. It was a later edition, and the story of the murder of O'Brien and Calvert still occupied the greater part of the front page. There was a report that it was believed Calvert was wanted by the English police; there was a story of two men, one probably English, seen near the house, and also of an Irishman with a beard. There was also an interview with O'Brien's gardener and his maid.

Snub sat in a corner, digested it, and then said: "Things are hotting up. You don't think there's much more to cover here, you say?"

"I don't," said Rollison.

"I suppose not. The smuggling, the booty and the fact that O'Brien was buying Majors' shares—that seems about the lot. Er—except one thing. Rumble's still here. Will he risk his neck in England again?"

"It's as safe there as here," said Rollison. "I don't think he'll stay in Dublin." He laughed a little, as if to himself, before he added, "Now I'll telephone Grice and then we'll get back, Snub."

Grice was not at his office. Rollison left a message, and Snub returned from the telephone to report that there was no chance of getting a seat on the evening plane. There was one for the first plane next morning, and one on the afternoon flight.

Rollison said: "I don't think we'd better wait, we'll be able to charter a special. Fix it, will you?"

Snub went off again, and while he was away there was a telephone call for Rollison. He hurried to his room and took the call there. It was Grice; and Rollison felt that he was transported back to London and the sight of Peter Lund on that pale-blue carpet.

Grice said quietly: "So you are all right?"

"Nicely, thanks. How are tricks?"

"What do you know about it?" asked Grice, speaking most guardedly.

Rollison chuckled. "Not guilty," he said. "Bill, Chloe Romeo's family have cleared out of their home and taken her brother, who has a big beard, with them."

"He's in London," said Grice. "We've got him at Cannon Row, and his family is being watched. He flew by special plane, and we picked him up after an SOS from Dublin—he was seen near O'Brien's house, you know. Hadn't you better come back?"

"Just as fast as an aeroplane will bring me," promised Rollison.

The journey took three hours – including the run out to Collinstown – and, a little more than an hour after they had arrived at Croydon, Rollison was sitting with Grice at Scotland Yard and Snub was on his way to the flat. Grice, looking hot and bothered, dropped into a chair and shook his head wearily at Rollison.

"What *have* you been up to?"

"Dodging bullets," said Rollison and told him the story, omitting no detail.

Grice seemed more cheerful when he had finished. Dublin had been in touch with him, he said; he had been on the phone to the Dublin police for the better part of an hour. He had reported his interest in O'Brien and confessed to having a man watching him at the post office. The Irish police were not too pleased about that, Grice added, and laughed.

"They certainly wouldn't be if they knew whom you'd sent," said Rollison.

"Oh, I had someone else there," Grice said. "He missed you and O'Brien while trying to fellow the pedestrian Rumble."

"Ah, I wondered when we'd get to your Rumble," Rollison smiled.

"He tells an odd story," Grice said. "The whole family is supported by Romeo, and jumps to his orders – or requests! The bearded brother-in-law said he was telephoned by Romeo to be at O'Connell Bridge—"

"When the other bearded man robbed O'Brien," said Rollison.

"Yes. He was also told to go to O'Brien's house, to meet Romeo. Romeo didn't turn up, he grew tired of waiting, and went off. As he was walking to the bus a taxi passed him. Inside was his own double."

"I think that's true," Rollison said. "What does Romeo say?'"

"He denies sending any message to his brother-in-law."

"Why did the family leave?"

"Again, officially on instructions from Romeo, who denies that, too. I don't know quite what to make of it, Rolly."

Rollison said slowly: "Someone might be framing Romeo, you know."

"I think Romeo's involved," said Grice, "but something has turned up. O'Brien was buying Majors' shares presumably on Calvert's instructions. Behind it all there is, I think, the feud between Calvert and Romeo. I shall be surprised if Romeo is paying Rumble."

"My Rumble?"

"Oh, the brother isn't your Rumble. He hasn't been out of Ireland for months. He's a Fabian with a Shaw-complex, hence his beard."

"Which my Rumble finds a help," said Rollison. "Well, now, can you tell me anything about Alice Hellier?"

Grice said slowly: "No, she's vanished. Your aunt is very upset. You know, in a case like this you shouldn't have used the old lady."

Rollison raised an eyebrow and refused to be side-tracked.

"What's happened to the Yard, Bill? Wasn't Alice watched?"

"She slipped my man," said Grice.

"Or is that the man's excuse?"

"There were two men," Grice said. "We weren't taking any chances. She knew she was being followed and chose the right moment to slip across the road and disappear into the subway at Piccadilly. She risked her neck doing it," Grice went on. "There's no doubt at all that she didn't want to be followed. I know you don't like rating her as a suspect, Roily, but there's never been a satisfactory explanation of her encounter with you, has there?"

"No," admitted Rollison.

Grice put his elbows on the desk and leaned forward.

"And she was at Greengates when Peter Lund was murdered."

"Ah."

"I shouldn't try to laugh it off," Grice said sharply. "It must be considered. On your own admission she's shown remarkable coolness when she was attacked, and a curious thing happened at Greengates. She was chloroformed, and it was administered so carefully that it didn't burn her nose or mouth at all. She might have been unconscious when you found her, but not necessarily for long. She could have been a party to the murder." Grice was aggressive now, and stabbed a forefinger at Rollison.

"All granted," said Rollison cheerfully. "Alice has a lot to explain. But Calvert *did* try to shoot her. I saw that, too."

"Did he try? Or did he only pretend to try?"

"I think that's going a bit far," said Rollison. "Anyhow, what are the facts? Calvert, O'Brien and Peter Lund are dead and I mourn only one. The first two were concerned in buying Majors' shares; the smuggled furs and jewels were addressed to Peter at Majors, which involved him. It also suggests that Peter wasn't straight, and—"

"Rolly, Peter Lund was *not* straight," Grice said. "I know he was a friend of yours, and I know you won't like admitting it, but there it is."

Rollison said: "I know, Bill. Calvert and O'Brien and Peter were involved in the smuggling. I've realised that since I went to O'Brien's house. But there was something else on Peter's mind; he didn't come to me because his conscience sent him."

"I think he came to you because he fell out with Calvert. He didn't at first want us told, remember," Grice was crisp now. "There are two crimes, Rolly. The smuggling and selling through Majors with or without Romeo's connivance; and the attempt to get control of Majors."

"I'll grant you both," Rollison agreed. "I think Romeo might have connived at the smuggling but that he's innocent of the other, bigger business. Therefore I think he's innocent of any conspiracy with Rumble. Now, here's a suggestion. The rogues fell out—Peter, Calvert and Rumble. Peter blotted his copybook by coming to see me, doubtless because he was frightened of being murdered. Calvert was in charge of the Dublin end. Rumble killed them both, at the same time killing the smuggling, but – and this is important – silencing all who knew his real identity and leaving a clear field for his battle with Romeo. Follow me?"

"So far," Grice said.

"Good! Calvert wanted those drawings and took risks to have them posted to Ireland. Rumble also wanted them, which makes them important. But Rumble knew they were going to be at the Dublin post office – or that they might be. How did he find out?"

"I don't know," said Grice.

Rollison said: "Name Rumble's informant and you'll soon find Rumble. And remember that Romeo didn't know. Now, another thing. Rumble wanted to get me as well as Calvert and O'Brien at the Dundrum house. In that, and only in that, his plans failed."

"Yes," said Grice, "but Romeo knew of the house, according to Hilary."

"You need to question Romeo about that," Rollison interrupted. "When will you tackle him?"

"In the morning," Grice said. "He's gone north with his wife. I gave him permission to go in the hope that he does something silly. So far it's been a normal business trip, I had a message only an hour ago."

"I see," said Rollison. "I'd like to be with you when you see him."

"I'll see what I can do," promised Grice.

The evening and the night passed uneventfully.

Rollison went to the flat to find Jolly there alone. Snub had gone out for a drink, and Jolly implied, without putting it into words, that he was troubled about Snub.

Rollison said slowly: "Snub's fallen for Alice Hellier, and is scared stiff in case she's involved."

"I *see,* sir," said Jolly.

"And Grice thinks she may be," Rollison went on. "I'm afraid we've got to admit that Peter Lund went wrong."

"I'm very sorry about that, sir," said Jolly. "It fully explains his behaviour. Higginbottom has brought me up to date with everything. May I ask if you think Miss Hellier knew about Mr. Lund and was, in fact, a party to the smuggling?"

"I don't want to think it," Rollison said. "We'll see. Now, what about your new job?"

"I have little to report," Jolly said. "The dispatch department is the one where there is most trouble, I think, but I will investigate further. Have you any other instructions?"

After a pause, Rollison said: "Yes, Jolly. Those smuggled goods had to be hidden somewhere. You might find a hiding-place."

"I will do all I can, sir," promised Jolly. The night was uneventful. Rollison went early to Majors, and one of the first people he saw when he entered with Grice was Jolly. Jolly was being helpful to two old ladies, who beamed upon him and went on their way. A slip of a girl behind a counter called to him gaily. Jolly turned towards her, his manner changing from the deferential to the authoritative.

Store detectives and men from the Yard were on duty at the store, one on each floor. Rollison saw them as the lift passed, and three of the men spotted Grice and tried desperately to acknowledge him as the lift went upwards. Grice studiously avoided them and talked to Rollison. Romeo had returned by air, Chloe had gone to Chelsea and Romeo had come straight here.

They reached the top floor and walked across the office, which was tidy again. The tight-lipped woman hurried towards them and actually greeted Grice with a smile. Then she recognised Rollison, and the smile disappeared. Rollison beamed at her.

Hilary was coming out of an office, and stopped abruptly.

"Hallo," he said, his voice pitched on a high key. "Have you seen him?"

"Romeo?" asked Grice sharply.

"Yes. I can't find him anywhere," said Hilary, "and everyone seems to want him at once. It's an astonishing thing," he added; "the shares opened very weak this morning, less than ten shillings, but someone's buying really fast. They're up to fifteen and a half. I *must* find Romeo. I don't know what I ought to do."

"Buy," said Rollison.

"That's all very well. If the other directors"—Hilary lowered his voice and glanced nervously over his shoulder—"were worth a row of beans it would be all right, but without Romeo they just sit round and cackle."

"What time did Romeo leave?" asked Grice sharply.

Hilary stared.

"He hasn't been in."

"He has. He was followed here," Grice said, and his voice grew sharper. "Hasn't he been up here?"

"The whole staff is looking for him," declared Hilary, with some exaggeration. "He *can't* have been here."

Grice said, "Wait here, Rolly."

He hurried downstairs again, and Hilary shrugged his shoulders and took Rollison into his office. He made no comment about what had happened in Ireland, and looked really harassed. His eyes were bloodshot, as if he had slept very little, and his hands were working. Now and again he yawned, tried to cover it, and eventually laughed rather bitterly.

"I can't carry the whole store," he complained.

"I shouldn't try to," said Rollison. "I—"

The telephone bell rang. Hilary lifted the receiver, scowled, said that Romeo was not in, and then listened.

"Oh, all right, I'll come along," he said at last. "I won't be a minute," he added to Rollison; "the fourth floor-manager wants to see me." He hurried out of the office and Rollison heard him hurrying along the passage.

Rollison looked about the room, and at the little window that gave into Romeo's office.

It was ajar, and that surprised him, although he hardly knew why. It had been closed when Romeo had been in the office. He went to the window and as he reached it he heard a sound from the other side. He stood still. *Was* Romeo in his office, and had he told Hilary to put off any callers? It was the kind of trick which Romeo would try, and be amused because he was sitting in his office all the time.

Rollison could see only a part of a blank wall. He stood quite still. There were no other sounds except that of someone breathing. There followed a footfall, so soft that he might almost have imagined it. Then he saw a shadow appear against the wall, as the sun came out and shone through Romeo's window. There was someone in the office, creeping towards the window. Rollison backed away and watched the shadow. The man next door reached it and put up a hand, which could be seen clearly through the glass. He pulled at the little window, which gave a slight squeak and the hand disappeared.

Rollison stood quite still.

The hand appeared again, and the window was opened; it did not squeak this time. A man with a spade-shaped beard appeared and looked through the window; and in his right hand he held a gun.

Chapter Twenty-Two

Frayed Nerves

Rollison knelt down and began to move slowly on his hands and knees; thus he could get past the window without being seen, and could reach the door of Romeo's room. The man with the gun was after either him *or* Hilary. Rollison was immediately beneath the window when he squinted up and saw the beard immediately above his head. The temptation to put up his hand and tug it was almost irresistible, but he forced it back; that beard would almost certainly come off. He got safely past and, still by the wall, stood up.

Then he heard Grice say from the passage: "Of course, he's here!"

The beard disappeared in a flash. A door opened. Grice exclaimed; a woman cried, *"Look!"* in a high-pitched voice and Grice shouted. Running footsteps sounded, followed by the slamming of a door. Grice shouted again, men came rushing towards the door and Rollison hurried into the passage. He could see Grice and the tight-lipped woman, who was half-way into Romeo's office. Grice was rushing towards the wall in the corner.

Hilary's voice came breathlessly from one of the offices: "Now what's all this?"

Grice shouted: "There's a door here! Where does it lead?"

"Door? What door?" demanded Hilary, appearing from a doorway.

"Oh, there is!" the woman cried. "In the comer, I saw it close, I saw it. And—the man with the gun. With the gun!"

Rollison went into the room and Hilary pushed after him, Two or three other men were jammed in the doorway. Grice was examining the wall. There appeared to be no doorway, but there were wooden panels by which a secret door might easily be concealed. Grice was running his fingernails up and down and along the panels. He spoke over his shoulder to Hilary.

"Do you mean to tell me you didn't know about this?"

"Of course I didn't!"

Grice found the spring almost at once; there was a control switch at the top of a panel, and when he touched it the door swung open slightly. It led to a narrow staircase and with Grice in the lead they filed down it. It was dark and gloomy, reminiscent of the house at Dundrum.

The steps stopped at what appeared to be a blank wall.

"Well I'm damned!" exclaimed Hilary.

Rollison said, "That looks like a hole." He bent down and put his eye to a small hole, not half an inch in diameter, about on a level with his waist. He stayed there for a moment, then saw a seat—

He straightened up, grinning.

"What—" began Hilary.

Rollison said, "It's the toilet."

Grice put up his hand to a switch above his head and pulled it. A door in the wall opened and they found themselves in a tiny compartment. Rollison opened the door, leading to a larger cloakroom. On the floor was a coat, a pair of cotton gloves and a trilby hat.

"We mustn't forget that he's still got his gun and beard," said Rollison. "Here, he could look through the spy-hole and make sure it wasn't occupied. If he knew he wanted to use it he could keep that compartment locked. It's only just big enough for our Romeo. Not bad, Bill!"

"The gunman might have got out of the office this way but he didn't get out of the store," said Grice heavily. "Every exit is watched. And Romeo hasn't been seen since he came in an hour and a half ago."

"I tell you he hasn't been *in* the office," insisted Hilary, stubbornly. "And he wouldn't come into the store without—"

"He's been in!" snapped Grice.

"And hasn't gone out by any of the main exits," pointed out Rollison. "Did you think of the dispatch department?" he asked.

"Of course."

"If he came in he must still be in," said Hilary.

"I wonder," said Rollison. "There's a garage, isn't there?"

"Yes, but—"

"I tell you it was watched!" snapped Grice.

"For Romeo, yes. Did your men have instructions to examine all vans which left the place?"

Rollison was already hurrying towards the lift and the others followed, Grice silent now. They reached the packing department, went through it to the dispatch department, which was a little above ground level. Dozens of men and girls were busy. There were no doors at one end, only a platform against which several vans were drawn, silver vans with a black 'Majors' painted on either side.

Hilary spoke in a hoarse voice.

"He—he *did* sometimes go out with a van, he—"

Grice turned to a grey-haired man standing by, with 'Foreman' written in a badge on his overall.

"Have you seen Mr. Romeo this morning?"

"Why yes, sir. He went out with Grey—"

"Give me that van number," Grice said abruptly. "Tell me what round it was supposed to be doing."

"Hurry!" snapped Hilary.

Rollison held his peace, knowing that Grice was fully aware that Romeo could easily have gone to earth and might have been kidnapped by the vanman.

A careful check in the next two hours proved that Grey, a comparatively new vanman, had delivered nothing that morning. The van was found on Wimbledon Common early in the afternoon, with the goods untouched but without the driver or his director. On the Common, where Romeo and his wife took romantic strolls, Romeo had disappeared.

The hunt was up for him.

Chloe, who received Grice and Rollison sweetly, was puzzled but not worried. It was not unusual for Augustus to go away for a few days and she was sure that the police need not be alarmed. She sat in the drawing-room, which had now been freed by the police, looking demure and lovely, and irritating Grice by her placidness. Rollison held only a watching brief.

"I see, Mrs. Romeo," said Grice, restraining himself from sharpness. "Now I would like you to tell me this: how often did you and Mr. Romeo go to Wimbledon Common for—er—a walk?"

"Sometimes once, sometimes twice a week," answered Chloe.

"Were you always alone?"

She smiled sweetly. "Yes, Mr, Grice. That's why we went there."

Rollison hid a smile.

"On no occasion did you meet anyone by appointment?"

"Certainly not. Why should we?" she asked.

"Did you always go to the same place?"

"We always left the car at the Green Man and just walked," declared Chloe, raising her eyes ever so slightly, as if to convey the sense of rapture.

Grice bit his lips, and Rollison broke a long silence.

"I wonder if Mrs. Romeo would come with us to the Common, Bill? She might be able to—"

"That wouldn't help!" snapped Chloe, showing signs of heat, but she quickly calmed down. "I mean, how *would* it help, Mr. Rollison?"

"Because we have a theory that Mr. Romeo has lost his memory," Rollison told her, keeping a straight face, "and he may have wandered to the spots which he loved so well." Grice shot him a quick, curious glance.

The woman looked doubtful.

"I don't think it likely that he has lost his memory," she said. "I don't think Augustus would do anything like that. But if you would really like me to come—"

Grice said quickly, "We would, Mrs. Romeo."

"All right, then, I'll be ready in five minutes," she promised and hurried out of the room, treating them to a radiant smile as she opened the door.

The moment it was closed Grice turned and demanded: "What are you getting at?"

"Ruffling Chloe," answered Rollison, promptly. "She was already slightly ruffled, but smoothed her feathers pretty quickly. Have you ever heard anything like it? She acts the simpleton all the time, she doesn't seem to know that you *want* Romeo. She's just too simple to believe."

"I'm coming to that conclusion myself," agreed Grice. "But what good will it do to take her to Wimbledon Common?"

"Apparently it was a trysting-place and held associations for them," answered Rollison, "and we might get a line. If they were at Wimbledon Common the night that Peter was murdered they were probably tricked into going there—to meet someone. The place might have guilty associations, too."

"Oh, you're as vague as she is," Grice said testily.

"She's far too definite," corrected Rollison. "Anything's worth trying now," he added, "because when it gets round that Romeo's missing, Majors' shares will start falling like a stone." Ha laughed. "A tricky business!"

The trip to the Common was abortive. They walked and drove about, and Chloe said that she and Romeo sometimes walked here and sometimes walked there. The men searching the Common, the evidence that the hunt was up for Romeo, did not seem to impress her at all. Rollison watched her closely, but not once did he find that she showed any emotion at all except a simple pleasure.

While they were there, Inspector Bray came to report to Grice. The inspector was in a dour mood. There were no footprints to and from the van, nothing at all which would help them to trace Romeo — and he reminded Grice that it was possible that Romeo and the driver were on the other side of London.

"Anyone could have brought the van here," Bray declared. "We can't find a soul who saw it arrive—not a soul."

"Keep looking," urged Grice.

The early evening papers carried the story — unauthorised but accurate — that the police were anxious to interview Augustus Romeo and the driver of a Majors' van, named Edward Grey. The newspapers were published an hour before the Stock Exchange closed and in the hour which followed there was a catastrophic drop in the value of the shares.

Rollison reached the flat at four o'clock and found Snub almost beside himself.

"Thank the Lord you've come!" Snub greeted. "I've had a heck of an afternoon. Your broker's been on the line every five minutes. Do you still want him to buy? He wanted you to start unloading and I told him you would have told me if you wanted that. Er—I hope I've done right."

"What have you done?"

"Told him to keep buying." Snub looked at Rollison from narrowed eyes. Obviously it had been a strain, for he was pale and his eyes were bloodshot — rather like Hilary's that morning — and his hair was on end. He paused before he went on in a low voice: "You know, you pretty well own Majors by now."

"That's a slight exaggeration," Rollison said.

"Supposing it *does* go broke," muttered Snub.

Rollison laughed. "Then so will we! But Majors won't go smash. Get the brokers for me," he went on.

Two minutes later he was talking to the harassed broker, who shouted when he introduced himself and went on shouting and asked him whether he wanted to drive him, the office and everyone connected with him mad. He *must* be mad to buy Majors, they were down to five shillings. The recovery hadn't stood up to the strain of Romeo's disappearance. Rollison was—

"Is anyone else buying?" interrupted Rollison.

"There *was* a sudden spate at the end of the day, but it was too late to stop the fall," said the broker. "It's one of the biggest rackets *I've* ever met, and one or two reputations are going to be broken over this. Including yours, if you're not careful."

"What makes you say that?" demanded Rollison.

"Do you need telling? The City knows you're buying."

"Why the devil did you let them know?"

"*I* didn't let them!" squealed the broker. "The story was spread about. I thought you'd done it to try to bolster up the market. Instead of that—look here, Rollison, if this does hit bottom it will knock you pretty badly, won't it?"

"That's putting it mildly."

"Well, I warned you," said the broker, more quietly. "I don't know who else was buying at the end of the day—it wasn't Dublin—but unless they're prepared to come into the market early in the morning and buy heavily, you're sunk."

"I'm not sunk until Majors is sunk," Rollison told him. "Hold until I tell you to sell," he added, firmly.

"It looks as if I'll have to," said the broker, and then went on seriously. "There's another angle that you haven't noticed, probably. All the small holders have sold out. A lot of people have lost small fortunes and it will become a first-class city scandal. That's where your danger lies. If it's thought that you've helped to engineer this—"

"Don't be an ass!"

"*I'm* not responsible for what other people might think," said the broker, "I'm just warning you that your name may stink before morning."

He rang off, and Rollison sat back in his chair and thought gloomily about the situation. His gloom was deepened when, at half past five, Jolly came in carrying a sheaf of evening papers. He greeted Rollison primly, and left the papers on the desk. That was not done without a purpose, and Rollison picked them up. Each starred the Majors sensation and each gave emphasis to the fact that the Hon. Richard Rollison was known to be buying shares heavily.

"That's caused it," muttered Rollison.

The telephone soon began to ring. Snub, Jolly and Rollison answered it in turn. Friends, relatives, acquaintances and complete strangers rang to ask whether Rollison could give them any advice about Majors shares. At least four acquaintances and two strangers threatened violence. It grew more and more obvious that Majors debacle was spreading alarm and despondency throughout the small shareholders. By evening, the morning newspapers were telephoning or at the door; Snub had thought himself frantic during the afternoon but now seemed to be standing on his head. At least he had little time to think of Alice. Throughout all this Jolly remained as prim and polite as ever, but towards the end of the evening perspiration was standing out on his forehead, and it was clear, when he looked at Rollison, that he thought the big mistake had been made at last.

There was no news of Romeo or Alice.

Hilary looked in, delivered himself of a homily suitable to a man of sixty, and went out, saying surprisingly that whatever anyone said he did not believe that Romeo would do anything crooked. His last cryptic remark was that if he were the police he would want to know what Chloe Romeo knew about this.

He rang the bell again immediately after he had left, and when Jolly opened the door, he strode in and pushed the door of the living-room wide open, Rollison was standing and looking at the trophy wall, for a measure of comfort. He glanced over his shoulder.

"What, you again?"

"I've remembered what I really came about now," said Hilary. "I'm so worried I hardly know whether I'm on my head or my heels. Er—is there any news of Alice Hellier?"

"Not yet."

Hilary clenched his fists.

"What *are* you playing at? I thought the Toff was pretty hot; after this I'll have a different opinion! She came to you for help and so did Peter. So did Romeo, for that matter, and you've let 'em all down. If that kid is killed—"

"Alice?"

"Who else do you think I'm talking about?" snapped Hilary.

"Do you know her well?"

"I know her well enough to know she's a damned fine woman and she deserves better of you than *this!*" cried Hilary. He was almost beside himself, waving his arms about and glaring at Rollison. Snub was a keenly interested spectator from the door, and Jolly was still talking on the telephone. "If any harm comes to that girl it'll be your fault, and don't you forget it!"

"I won't," said Rollison, quietly.

"I tell you it's driving me crazy," muttered Hilary, suddenly lowering his voice. "I can't stand it, Rollison. Alice—Romeo—Peter. And—and I can't understand you." He lowered himself to the arm of a chair and stared at Rollison, who glanced towards the cocktail cabinet — a silent order to Snub, who immediately poured drinks. "It's a fact that you're buying heavily in Majors' shares, it's all over London. And it's a damned queer thing, Rollison."

"What is?"

"You know what I mean. You buying like this—especially after you've failed to help the others."

"Now have a little drink," soothed Snub.

"Damn you, don't talk to me like that!" cried Hilary. He jumped up, and Snub snatched the glass away just in time to save it from being knocked out of his hand. "This whole set-up is phoney. I wouldn't trust any of you out of my sight!"

He swung round and rushed across the room. Snub cocked an eye, Rollison nodded, and Snub left the flat a moment after Hilary. Jolly had opened the door without a word to allow the youngster to storm out, and again to let Snub out.

Snub hurried down the stairs, soft-footed. He could hear Hilary reach the street. Hilary slammed the front door behind him, which cut off most sound. Snub hurried on, opened it, and heard footsteps. He went into the street and turned right — and a man leapt out of the shadows and struck at him savagely.

Chapter Twenty-Three

Rumble's Triumph

A few minutes after Snub had left, the telephone in the flat rang again. Rollison motioned to Jolly to take the call and paused near the hat-stand. Jolly's expression suffered a remarkable change as he listened, and he waved a hand excitedly to Rollison.

Rollison heard a vague, "Hold on."

Jolly covered the mouthpiece with his hand, and whispered: "A man *said* that Rumble wants to speak to you, sir."

"Rumble, by George!" Rollison took the receiver and said: "Hallo." There was no immediate answer. The pause lengthened, and Jolly, already at the other instrument in the kitchen, where he had a direct line, was dialling Whitehall 1212. Rollison heard him ask for Grice or Bray, and then heard him say: "Someone is telephoning Mr. Rollison at the moment. I think it would be an advantage if the call were traced." There was a pause. "I understand that Rumble … Thank you, sir."

He rang off and hurried back to the hall.

"Mr. Grice is looking after it, sir."

"Good," said Rollison. "I—Hallo." Someone spoke near the other end, and then a voice so familiar with its deep rollicking note smote his ear.

"Rollison?"

"Speaking."

"And even sounding calm and collected," chuckled Rumble, "I hand it to you in some ways, Rollison, although not in others—why don't you give up detecting and take up marbles?"

"Some people prefer picking oakum," said Rollison.

"And smart, too! *I'm* a little too smart for oakum-picking." Rumble sounded as if he were delighted with himself. "You haven't shone, Rollison—in fact the Toff's admirers will think he's failed them for once. Have you seen the evening papers?"

"Yes."

"Bold, bad Toff running a racket so that he can cash in on the losses of the poor," chuckled Rumble. "Has that struck you before?"

"It's almost as if someone wants that to get around," said Rollison, brightly.

"You're getting back to form," observed Rumble. "Well, your name will be mud in the morning. And there'll be a bit of a scramble at Majors, I fancy. Shall I tell you a little story?"

"Drawing-room?" murmured Rollison.

"Of course, it's over the telephone. Ready? ... Good! For some time past I've been working up dissatisfaction at Majors by employing, through Calvert, a few agitators who've spread disaffection, not to mention incivility, all about them. Now I've spread the story that the store's going broke. Tomorrow morning there should be quite a scene, because the staff won't want to go without its salary. They knew it was rocky on pay day, because the cash went round late. Neat, isn't it?"

"That part of it is fairly good," conceded Rollison.

"Wait until you hear the rest! Shareholders in Majors are hopping mad. Naturally they blame Romeo, but thanks to rumour, the lying jade, they also blame you. Picking the pockets of the poor—"

"You're repeating yourself," Rollison reminded him.

"I never could resist alliteration! And I wouldn't be surprised if there isn't what the newspapers call an angry mob outside Majors in the morning. There might also be an angry mob outside Gresham Terrace."

"I see," said Rollison.

"Do I detect a little glumness of voice?" asked Rumble, and he chuckled deep in his throat. "Let me depress you further. I am not Chloe's brother, I used him as a stooge because of his beautiful beard. It served me well and it served to confuse Romeo, who would do anything for his Chloe and her family."

"Why tell me all this?" asked Rollison.

"My dear chap! You deserve to know. But I mustn't stay much longer. When the police arrive one of my men will warn me and we'll slip away—you needn't have wasted time telling them to trace the call." He chuckled again. "Poor Peter, poor Alice, and poor, poor Romeo," he added. "Romeo won't dare to show his face again. Majors will have changed hands and someone will be sitting pretty, because that store's as sound as a bell."

"I'm sitting pretty," said Rollison.

Rumble said: "You think you are. But the public won't like it. You may have some quixotic notion such as selling back at the price they sold for, but they'll tear you limb from limb before you've got time to explain it. Take a tip from me, Rollison. The directors at Majors are a pretty spineless lot, but they'll make you an offer for your shares. Take it."

"Or what?" asked Rollison.

"You've taken the point neatly," said Rumble. "If you don't play, you won't see Alice or Romeo again. Romeo will commit suicide. I've thought out a new method which even the police won't see through. His wife will then be sitting pretty, won't she? Have I ever told you what I think of his wife?"

"I don't want to hear," said Rollison. "Don't hurt Alice Hellier."

"I thought you had a chink in the old armour," said Rumble. "They'll both be hurt unless you sell out. I'm covered by the directors. I want to make a fat profit and I'll manage all right if you behave yourself. She's got lovely blue eyes, hasn't she?"

"Who?"

"Alice. Sorry, I must go, your friends are in the offing." Rumble rang off. Rollison replaced the receiver slowly and Jolly, who had been listening on the extension, joined him, but stood by without speaking. Rollison lit a cigarette, and shrugged his shoulders.

"He's got a nice manner for a murderer, hasn't he?"

"I suppose one could say so, sir."

"What are conditions like at Majors?"

"He has summed it up neatly, sir. I can place a finger on the trouble-makers. There is no great cause for dissatisfaction, just a series of minor irritations, as one might say, and they have been magnified out of all proportion. There was some talk this evening of the stores going into bankruptcy and some fears expressed about salaries lost."

"Cleverly managed," said Rollison. "And the agitators were employed by Calvert."

"Precisely, sir."

"And now we know that Rumble thinks he can make the directors do what he likes. We know he's been in a position to watch all that goes on there. The question again is—who is Rumble?" Rollison laughed. "What do you make of it?"

"I am a little alarmed for Miss Alice and, in a lesser degree, for Romeo," observed Jolly. "Have you any idea where she is?"

Rollison said: "Nothing firm. Jolly, I wonder if Romeo ever left that store. The packer foreman said—"

"That foreman left today, sir," murmured Jolly.

"Did he, by Jove?"

"And he and the man Grey, who was supposed to have driven Romeo off, were both trouble-makers," said Jolly. "I have been waiting for an opportunity to tell you about that. The atmosphere has been a little hectic tonight, sir."

"There ought to be a law against telephones," said Rollison. "So they've flown, and the packer lied. You know, the smuggled goods were handled by someone in the store; dispatch men would be useful for that. It's building up slowly. Have you found any hiding-place for the goods?"

"I have tried to search everywhere, sir," said Jolly. "I have not yet completed the fur *salon*, but I will be on duty early in the morning and I have arranged to take a spell of duty among the furs. That *is* a good hiding-place, sir, with so many cupboards and sliding doors, and if I find one—"

"You might find Alice and Romeo."

"We could suggest to the police that they search tonight," Jolly said.

"Grice will do that the moment he wants to," said Rollison. "Well, I think Romeo and Alice are safe, you know." Jolly made no comment. "I think Rumble will hold them as hostages in the hope of making me sell out my Majors' shares."

"That is my opinion, sir," said Jolly. "If I may say so, you made a very astute move when you began to buy. Although it might have some repercussions on your good name, that will soon be rectified, and Rumble is defeated of his ultimate object."

"To cash in—yes," said Rollison. "I—Hallo, who's that?" There was a sharp ring at the front-door bell.

Jolly went to answer it, and Grice strode in. He did not speak to either of them but went to the phone, picked it up and dialled a number. Two men were on the landing, and there was a whispered colloquy going on downstairs. Someone called on: "Is he bad?" and Rollison's eyes narrowed, but he did not speak. Grice, as if he deliberately wanted to tensify the atmosphere, held on while his call was being connected, and then spoke abruptly into the telephone: "St. David's Hospital … This is Superintendent Grice of New Scotland Yard … Will you send an ambulance to 23g Gresham Terrace, W.1, at once, please … Yes, an official call." He held on for a moment, grunted, "All right," and then rang off.

Neither Rollison nor Jolly moved or spoke.

Grice said: "We found Higginbottom just outside. It's touch and go. And that call to you from Rumble came from round the corner."

Rollison told Grice of the possibility that Romeo and Alice were at the stores, and Grice telephoned his inspector in charge there, giving him, instructions to make a search; clearly Grice expected to find bodies or nothing at all. All the people concerned, including Chloe and Hilary, were closely watched. An hour after Snub had been taken away, the report from the hospital was discouraging. Snub was on the operating-table and the chances were no more than fifty-fifty.

At midnight, Rollison and Jolly were alone in the flat.

"Shall I ring the hospital again, sir?" asked Jolly.

"It won't help. We'll ring first thing in the morning, Jolly."

"Yes, sir."

"There will probably be trouble at Majors and here. We'll both leave early. You'll go straight to the store, I'll go to see Grice. When you get there, whether the police have made a good job or not, search Majors somehow for a hiding-place. I can't help thinking that Romeo didn't leave the place."

"Perhaps we shall have word from Mr. Grice," said Jolly, hopefully.

There was no word.

At eight o'clock next morning a little crowd was gathered outside Gresham Terrace, and when Rollison left he was in no doubt as to the opinion of the people. The London newspapers had named him freely, and there was no mystery about it.

Jolly left for Majors, and Rollison saw Grice at the Yard. No results had come from the search of the stores. There was no news of either Romeo or Alice but there were fairly good tidings about Snub; be had come through the operation, and might recover completely. Cheered up by that, Rollison asked Grice: was he expected at Majors?

"I've prepared for the worst," said Grice. "We'll have a strong force there and a few mounted men. They'll be after Romeo's blood—*and* yours."

"I'll look after mine," said Rollison. "Are you coming?"

Great crowds outside the store were watching the staff arrive. Only the staff doors were open, but every other entrance was thronged with people, as if this were a remnant sale and Majors' goods were to go as cheaply as Majors' shares. Police, including some mounted men, were keeping watch. There was no trouble yet, although some of the crowd showed signs of anger, especially when well-dressed executives pushed their way through to the door.

Rollison watched from a window on a first floor opposite.

Jolly had already gone through and the crowd had closed about him. On the fringes of the throng a few scared girls were waiting. A policeman escorted them to the staff door. A fat man, fairly well dressed, got out of a car near Lawson Street, and immediately a cry went up.

"There's Romeo!"

It was not Romeo, but he was almost as large as the fat man. For the first time anger seared the crowd and there was a concerted rush towards the unfortunate, who looked round desperately as people pressed upon him. A mounted policeman set off to help, with three men walking behind him. The crowd surged back. The man they thought was Romeo was protecting his face with folded arms and trying to force his way through to the staff entrance. Men and women were snatching at his clothes and striking at him. Then the mounted policeman cleared a path and the fat man closed in behind the horse, with the three men on foot behind him.

Grice was standing by Rollison's side.

"Now you know what to expect," he said.

Rollison smiled. "It's grim, but I'm not fat!"

"If you were recognised, they'd be after you."

"We'll see," said Rollison. "I'm not so well known as that, you know."

"If you're going in, I'll have a guard for you," said Grice.

"Don't do that," urged Rollison. "I'd like to see what happens. You follow at a safe distance!" He turned and went downstairs, past Bray, who was watching anxiously. The crowd had seemed big from above, but at ground level it seemed much larger. Traffic was held up and there was a regular stream of people trying to get to other shops and offices at the back of the crowd. Rollison stood watching for a few minutes. There were several men standing idly at the fringe, looking at the people as they passed.

"Watch those fellows," Rollison said.

"Who?" asked Grice.

Rollison pointed out a hefty-looking man wearing a muffler who was standing in a shop doorway, and two others, just on the edge of the crowd but, unlike everyone else, looking away from Majors.

"They're looking for someone," Rollison said. "I think I can guess who."

Grice said, "You're a fool if you try it."

"Just watch them," advised Rollison.

He walked past the man in the muffler; and as the fellow set eyes on him he stiffened. Rollison appeared to notice nothing and thrust his way through the fringes of the crowd so that the other men he had pointed out could see him. Their eyes narrowed, one looked at the other quickly and raised a hand. Grice must have seen all that. Rollison began to thrust his way towards the centre of the crowd. It was comparatively silent now, as if it had exhausted itself by the show of hostility towards the fat man.

Then a stentorian bellow sounded high above the murmurs of talk.

"There's Rollison!"

"Rollison!"

"There he is!"

He was hemmed in, the men were shouting one against the other, and one of them pushed his way through and reached his side. He struck at Rollison's face and shouted: "Take that, you swine!"

"There's Rollison!"

From a long way off, Grice shouted: "Come back! Come back!"

Rollison fended off the man and went headlong into the crowd, but the three followed him, bellowing until the rest of the crowd near could be in no doubt as to who was Rollison. Then the shouting became a roar on an ugly menacing note. Rollison straightened up, using his elbows as the crush grew worse, for from all sides the crowd had turned towards him. Someone threw a stone, a folded newspaper was slapped across his face; someone with an *Echo*, which had his photograph, screamed: "That's him!"

The three men who had started the cry had lost themselves in the crowd now. Policemen's helmets were showing above the serried mass of heads. Mounted police had been called but could not get through quickly; they made the crush about Rollison even greater. He had to get through. He had taken this chance and proved what he had set out to prove, but now the crowd was viciously angry. How many were shareholders, how many were trouble-makers and how many were sightseers he could not guess, but danger threatened from every side, from every hand. A fist caught him in the side of the chin but be ignored it and, still using his elbows, drew nearer to the front of the shop. Policemen were getting closer. Now and again Rollison thought he heard Grice's voice; had Grice made sure that the trouble-makers were detained?

A stick was banged on the back of his head.

It was no use fighting, he must run the gauntlet of shouting, waving, threatening people. Majors seemed a long way off and the crowd was even thicker here. Buffets and blows were coming from all directions.

A knife flashed in front of his eyes.

He saw the little man who wielded it. It flashed again, missing him by several inches. He felt sure that it was intended to miss, it was meant to frighten him. Since Rumble's call the night before that had been the great aim – to frighten him into selling his shares privately, cheaply. Someone had planned this to make a fortune out of Majors, and he had stopped them by buying too much. They stood to lose, not gain.

A woman screamed. A man with a walking-stick caught Rollison's neck in the crook, and he felt a rush of panic. He bent forward, managed to get the stick away, snatched it and began to swung it round. The crowd swayed away from him shouting his name. "Rollison! Rollison! Rollison!" It was reaching a crescendo of venom and bitterness, and the stick he wielded incensed them further.

How long would the police be?

Police-whistles began to pierce the air, sounding above the roaring. He glanced over his shoulder and saw two helmets not far away, and a mounted man a little to his left. There was a dangerous surge. He was pressed on all sides, his chest seemed crushed, he could hardly breathe …

And then the crowd swayed back and he was standing with the police about him.

They led him to the door. It was barricaded inside and out, and policemen were on duty just inside the entrance. The barricades were taken down and Rollison was pushed through. The crowd was still shouting, but as the doors closed the noise was reduced to an incoherent murmuring. Police and staff looked at him curiously as he stood breathing hard, his coat torn in several places his face scratched, a slight cut bleeding above his injured eye. He was so relieved at being out of the crush that he thought of little else; and the first thing he became aware of was Jolly.

"Will you come with me, sir, please?"

"Eh—oh, hallo, Jolly!"

"This way, sir, please," said Jolly.

"Er—yes." Rollison looked at the sergeant in charge. "Tell Superintendent Grice I'll be back."

"Very good, sir."

Jolly led the way through a thinning crowd of the staff, and as they reached a counter half-way along the department he took out a cigarette, placed it in a holder, lit it and then handed the cigarette to Rollison.

Rollison smiled his thanks.

"I will find some other clothes for you, sir," said Jolly mildly. "The cloakroom is in there, if you would like to wash. Smith!" He called to a youth who was standing by. "Take Mr. Rollison into the cloakroom and see that he has everything he wants."

"Yessir!"

Jolly came in ten minutes afterwards, with a lounge suit new from the peg. It was about the right size, he said, and helped Rollison to change. The suit fitted passably.

Rollison was refreshed and no longer breathless.

"Thanks, Jolly."

"I am very glad I was here, sir, after all. I think Mr. Grice is waiting for you."

"Good!"

Jolly led the way. Grice and Bray were near the entrance, but Rollison was less interested in them than in the three men – the trouble-makers – who were standing nearby, all of them handcuffed. Rollison's eyes brightened, but he ignored them as he reached Grice.

"I told you you were a damned fool," growled Grice; "you might have lost your life."

"But you wouldn't have caught those three beauties. Have they talked?"

"They were hired because they knew you from your East End jaunts," said Grice. "They were instructed just to shout your name and see that everyone else knew who you were. They were here the other night, too, keeping watch."

"On orders from—"

"Someone at Majors."

"Nice work," said Rollison. "Now all we want is that someone. I—" He broke off, because there was a disturbance at the far end of the department. He looked round and saw Hilary hurrying towards him, eager-faced, followed by Williams with the tuft of fair hair, and two or three other men whom Rollison vaguely remembered.

"Rollison!" exclaimed Hilary.

"And all in one piece," murmured Rollison,

"For the love of Mike, be serious! Rollison, we've been discussing this shocking position—"

"We?" asked Rollison.

Hilary snapped his fingers with annoyance, and Jolly, glancing at Rollison and catching his eye, began to move away.

"*Will* you be serious?" cried Hilary. "The directors and I have been discussing the position. This is Majors' responsibility. In Mr. Romeo's absence we can only do what we feel sure he would do in the circumstances—buy the shares back from you. That's the *only* thing to do."

"Not quite," Rollison said. "I can sell them back to the people who first unloaded them."

"Oh, don't be a fool!"

"But I bought them just for that purpose," Rollison said. He lit a cigarette and was aware of the tension which was sprung among them. "It's a curious thing, Hilary, but Rumble told me on the telephone that he wanted to buy my shares. Now you—"

"What the devil do you mean?" snapped Hilary.

"That you and Rumble have the same idea," said Rollison. "There are other curious similarities, too. The first time I met Rumble you had just left the office. The second time was in Dublin and you had just arrived. The third was at O'Brien's house and you arrived almost on his heels. The fourth was here, yesterday afternoon, when you went out of the office and Rumble appeared, with a gun, almost immediately afterwards. Odd, isn't it?"

Hilary gasped, "You must be mad!"

"The hidden staircase and the cloakroom were nicely placed for you to slip into or out of the beard and wig, the coat and gloves," said Rollison. "You've been close on my heels all the time, Hilary, and last night when Snub followed you he was brutally attacked—"

"I know nothing about it!"

"Oh, but you do," said Rollison. "Snub saw you."

Hilary screamed, "He couldn't have done!"

"Thanks very much," said Rollison, and Hilary realised the significance of what he had said.

Chapter Twenty-Four

Last Rumble

Grice motioned to his men and they moved forward, one taking Hilary's arm, the other flashing a pair of handcuffs. No one else moved or spoke. Hilary's face was working, he looked as if he would fling himself at Rollison; but he forced himself to speak.

"I'd be careful!"

"You haven't been quite careful enough."

"I'd be *very* careful," Hilary said. "Romeo and Alice Hellier—"

"Ah."

"I thought that would hurt you," sneered Hilary. "They're really behind it. I work for Romeo. But I've made sure they can't give evidence against me. They're locked in a room you'll never find. But if you let me go—"

Rollison said: "You've a queer idea of the working of the law, Hilary. You'll be charged and proved guilty, and you'll be hanged whether Alice Hellier and Romeo die or not. Nothing will save you from that and nothing will save your accomplice." Hilary drew in his breath.

"So I can hurt you, too," Rollison said. "Where's Romeo?"

Hilary stood silent.

Any other man than Grice would have interrupted then; but Grice stood silent, knowing there was something more on Rollison's mind, knowing that this was a battle between the two men and that an interruption would only do harm. Rollison forgot Grice and all the people about him, looked into Hilary's eyes and read the fear there.

He also felt afraid for Romeo and Alice.

He had suspected this man of being Rumble for some time; he had been sure that Hilary was more dangerous than Calvert and O'Brien, a callous and cold-blooded murderer without any normal standard of behaviour, who thought that he could bargain with the police for his own safety. Everything about Rumble had been abnormal; the danger, because of that, was greater than any.

Rollison said, "You'd better tell me, Hilary."

He did not use the word 'accomplice' again; he did not think that it was necessary. He wanted to make Hilary believe that he would be silent about others if the hiding-place of Romeo and Alice were disclosed.

Hilary might be persuaded.

There was a sudden flurry of footsteps at the far end of the big department, and Rollison glanced up, at first annoyed and then delighted, for Jolly was *hurrying* towards him and Jolly would hurry only in real emergency. Hilary swung round.

Jolly called: "I've found them, sir! I—"

"*Damn you!*" roared Hilary.

He kicked at the man who held him and snatched at his pocket. One man staggered, the other maintained his grip until Hilary jabbed an elbow into his face. Then the gun appeared in Hilary's hand, and he backed away.

"Keep back!" he cried.

Grice said loudly. "Don't be a fool, Hilary!"

Hilary cried again, "Keep back!" lie kept them covered, but must have known that some of Grice's men were coming towards him from behind. He backed to a showcase, rested a hand on it and vaulted over it. He fired at two men who were approaching and they ducked, then hesitated to attack. Grice moved forward. Hilary fired again, and Grice flinched.

"*Get back!*"

He turned and fired at another man between him and the door and then took to his heels, racing towards it. There were several men in the doorway. Rollison, Jolly, Grice and half a dozen others were moving in Hilary's wake, and saw him fire at the door. The glass smashed. The men in the porch backed away. Hilary pulled open the door and jumped outside. The crowd, pressing close to the windows, saw something of what was happening and involuntarily moved back.

Hilary turned just once.

Rollison saw his eyes turned towards him. Rollison ducked, and the bullet went over his head. Then Hilary leapt past men who grabbed at him, and plunged into the crowd. He fired twice into the air …

The crowd stampeded.

Rollison reached the door and saw the milling men and women terrified by fear which sent them in all directions at once. He heard the cries and shouts of the injured, saw a woman fall and disappear. He tried to keep Hilary in sight, but it was impossible; the man was swallowed up; there would be no finding him in the midst of this.

Grice was by his side.

"So he's made it," he said bitterly.

"He's got to go somewhere and it won't be to his home," Rollison said. The words sounded inane. "We'll try Greengates, I think." He turned to Jolly. "Well done, Jolly. The police will break down that wall if needs be. Stay on the spot, will you?"

"Yes, sir."

Grice was giving orders to Bray, who had just appeared, and not until he had finished did he speak to Rollison.

"What's this about Greengates?"

"It's the last place he'll expect us to look," Rollison said. "I'll tell you why on the way."

There were two policemen on duty at Greengates. No, Hilary had not been there that morning and Mrs. Romeo was still indoors. Rollison and Grice walked towards the front door, which was opened by Harold, the chauffeur. They went inside and Chloe came hurrying from the drawing-room.

"Have you brought news of my husband?" she asked.

"I'm afraid not just yet," said Rollison.

She looked childishly disappointed.

"Oh, I *am* vexed. And I'm worried, too, because I know how anxious he has been lately. Ever since he told my mother and the others to leave their home he's been on edge. I *do* hope he's not ill."

Grice said quickly: "*Did* he tell them to do that?"

"Oh yes," she said. "He told them they must leave at once. And he told my brother to go to a house in Dundrum, I heard him on the telephone. It's all so confusing."

"Yes, isn't it?" asked Rollison.

She looked at him sharply.

"*And* worrying. I really *am* distressed. I always thought Augustus was *a good* man, but now I don't know. Mr. Rollison, *is* he trying to get my brother into trouble?"

"Yes," said Rollison, promptly.

She raised her hands.

"Oh, that's too cruel! I can't allow it, I just can't!" She turned. "Do you mind coming with me?"

She did not wait for an answer but hurried up the stairs to a small study, immaculately neat and tidy. She went to the desk which was unlocked, and took out several books and some sheets of drawing-paper; and the sheets were covered with the childish drawings like those found in Calvert's office.

"Then I think you ought to see *these*," she said.

Grice and Rollison picked up the books.

There were accounts of the goods which had been brought from Ireland; and there were statements of Majors' shares recently bought in Ireland. Five minutes' scrutiny proved that those papers damned whoever owned them, both for a part in the smuggling and in the attempt to buy Majors' shares at rock-bottom prices.

Chloe said suddenly: "I *knew* there was something funny going on, I've been afraid of it. You see, Augustus hadn't very much money, he didn't own many shares in Majors and he wanted to get complete control. I don't pretend to understand it all, but I thought you ought to know. I wouldn't let him down before, but if he's trying to hurt my brother ..."

"That puts a different light on it," said Rollison.

"I'm so glad you understand!"

"Oh, I do," said Rollison. "I understand everything. So your husband had been behind all this. *Did* you go with him to Wimbledon on the night that Peter Lund was murdered?"

Chloe raised her hands to her breast.

"*Did* you?" demanded Grice sharply.

She looked distressed. "I promised him not to say anything but— no, *he* didn't, I went to Wimbledon alone; he left the car a little way from here. And he met someone there. He paid Harold fifty pounds not to say anything about it. And—and he's seen a lot of that girl, Alice Hellier. I'm not jealous, but—"

The phone rang across her words.

She glanced towards it.

"Oh, don't worry about that! Is Augustus—"

Rollison said, "I think we ought to answer it." He went to the telephone and lifted the receiver and said in a husky, rather effeminate voice: "Hallo, yes."

Hilary spoke.

"Chloe, get away at once. Don't wait for anything, meet me at London airport just before two o'clock, leave there at once."

"All right," said Rollison, in the same husky voice.

Hilary rang off.

Chloe came towards Rollison, her eyes sparkling.

"Why did you speak like that? Why did you pretend—"

Rollison said: "I spoke to Hilary, Mrs. Romeo, and he wants you to meet him at London airport just before two o'clock. You see, we *know* that Hilary is Rumble and we know you've been lying to us about your husband and Miss Hellier."

She did not speak.

"What we didn't know was whether we could prove that you and Hilary were involved together," Rollison said. "We can now. No, don't try to run away, you're going to be arrested."

Grice moved forward; and Chloe began to scream.

In essence it was simple, Rollison and Grice agreed. There were two distinct crimes – the smuggling and the tricks to get control of Majors. Rollison's earlier reasoning about the smuggling proved right, although they soon learned more. Calvert and Hilary had started it and then Peter had been persuaded to play a part – that fact had to be faced; and Peter Lund had always been wild, and on his globe-trotting had made many queer friends,

Calvert was one of them.

Out of the smuggling another plan had evolved – to get complete control of Majors. Peter had rebelled against that, but Calvert and Hilary had gone on with it, confident that Peter would not talk because he was so deeply involved. When he had gone to Rollison for help they had become alarmed, and they had watched not only Peter but Alice Hellier. A remark of Peter's had suggested that he had confided in Alice; Calvert had followed her, discovered her on the road with Rollison and, that night, tried to silence her.

He had sent the man to Bath, to frighten her into silence.

Once he had shown himself he had to fly. He had left Hilary in charge in London, after killing Peter. And Hilary, knowing that if the Dublin end were fully investigated the smuggling would be stopped, had seen a chance to clear himself and to leave the police believing that Calvert and Peter had been the only two concerned. So he had betrayed Calvert.

Earlier, he had created 'Rumble', aping Chloe's brother to spread confusion and false trails; and everything he and Chloe had done had been directed towards making Romeo seem responsible for the effort to corner Majors' shares. Even to the last Chloe had tried to do that.

Everything she had told Grice and Rollison was untrue; the papers were Hilary's, not Romeo's. Once she cracked, she cracked completely, and the whole story came out.

Romeo had first begun to suspect when he had discovered goods for sale which he had not purchased or allowed to be purchased, but Calvert had forced him to keep silent. Then he had discovered the secret of the crude drawings; one was sent from Dublin to Majors on the day that a fresh consignment of goods had been dispatched and, so that there could be no error, a similar crude drawing had been on the reverse side of the label. It was simple but effective, and Romeo had wanted the drawings to help break Calvert's influence.

Romeo and Alice were freed during that hectic morning. Romeo, not yet knowing the truth, was with Grice; and Alice was with Rollison in Hilary's office.

She looked tired after a long ordeal, for they had been given neither food nor drink, but she was frank enough now.

Rollison said, "Why *did* you come to me at the inn, Alice?"

"I felt that I had to find out what you know about Peter," she said, "I didn't much care about Peter but I—well, I love his mother. I wanted to save her from hurt. And I knew he had been doing something—something foolish. One night when he was frightened out of his wits lie told me what, and I—well, I *had* to keep silent."

"I see," said Rollison.

"But when he had the message from Romeo to go to Greengates you had to be told," Alice said, "that's why Snub came and joined us. It was Rumble – Hilary dressed up as Rumble, but I didn't know that then – who killed Peter. And he talked a lot. He was drunk with success. Rolly. I've never known an experience so—so horrid."

"I hope you won't again," said Rollison.

She shivered.

"He told me that he had sent Calvert after me on the road and told Calvert to try to kill me, and then he said he'd changed his mind about killing me, he said I would be more useful alive. And he told me to meet him at Piccadilly—the day I went there and avoided the police."

"Why did you do that?" asked Rollison.

She raised her hands.

"He told me that night that he would deal with Snub. I knew Snub was missing. I thought—Oh, I can't understand it, I don't pretend to, but Snub *matters*. I was afraid to tell the truth until I knew that he was safe."

"I see," said Rollison.

"Rumble said so much that night," said Alice. "He boasted that he had fixed Calvert, that you would be going to Dublin, that you would feel sure that Romeo was really behind it all. He said he hated Chloe Romeo ..."

"That was his favourite story, but he overdid it," Rollison said. "I've no doubt he sent her the red roses, but forgot to put his card with them."

"Red roses?" echoed Alice.

"It doesn't matter," said Rollison. "Well, now, a word in your ear. Snub's hurt, but he'll pull through, and although he can't understand it either, you *matter*."

There was radiance in her eyes.

There was no radiance in Grice's eyes when he came in a little later. Alice went into another room to tell her story officially, and Grice lit a cigarette.

"I've told Romeo," he said moodily, "and it's almost killed him. He's—just a broken man."

"He'll get over it," said Rollison, confidently.

"I'm not so sure. After seeing him, the details don't seem to matter, but ..."

He outlined the story as Rollison already knew it, and added one or two facts. Hilary had sent the little dark man to Romeo's office when Rollison had first been there, to shoot Rollison; by then Hilary was getting worried about the Toff. Darkie and White had worked for him, not knowing he was also Rumble: he had created the identity of Rumble so that he could discard it when it was no longer needed. He had decided to close up the Irish end, thinking it certain that Romeo would be suspected, and he had carefully planned to frame the fat man.

What he had not expected was that Rollison should buy Majors' shares; he himself had planned to buy them for next to nothing.

"And that was his weakness," Grice said; "he had to try to get them, talked the other directors into making that offer, and gave you the chance to spring what you knew on him. Why didn't you tell me what you thought?"

Rollison said: "There wasn't any proof. And I wasn't really sure of Alice's part, either, and I wanted to have it all cut and dried. Hilary's mistake was in using Chloe's brother—"

"Not a mistake," Grice said. "That was deliberate. The brother suspected that there was an *affaire* between him and Chloe. Hilary wanted him involved—and in arranging it became too involved himself. In fact," went on Grice, "the whole thing got too big for him, he would have been wiser to stick to the smuggling."

And Rollison agreed.

He went to see Romeo soon afterwards, and the man's pale face and tormented eyes hurt him; he understood what Grice had felt. Yet before the end of the day Romeo was perking up a little, worrying about what story would be told to the Press and how he would replace Peter Lund.

More cheerful than he had been for some time, Rollison went home. Jolly, who had promptly deserted his post at Majors, was waiting for him. Miss Hellier was calling shortly, she was now at the hospital with Higginbottom. Jolly hoped that all the truth was now known.

Rollison told him the story.

"I think we can congratulate ourselves, sir," remarked Jolly.

"*You* can," said Rollison.

"Mine was a trifling share, sir. I—Excuse me." He went to answer the telephone, which began to ring, and said into the mouthpiece: "This is the residence of ..." and then stopped.

"*Yes*, sir, he is in." He turned to Rollison. "It is Mr. Miller, sir."

"Miller?" Rollison took the receiver quickly.

"Rolly, we're absolutely stuck for the last match," said Miller from the West Country. "Can you possibly get down here by two o'clock tomorrow? We'll have to borrow a man if you can't."

"*That* won't do," said Rollison. "I'll be there."

John Creasey

Gideon's Day

Gideon's day is a busy one. He balances family commitments with solving a series of seemingly unrelated crimes from which a plot nonetheless evolves and a mystery is solved.

One of the most senior officers within Scotland Yard, George Gideon's crime solving abilities are in the finest traditions of London's world famous police headquarters. His analytical brain and sense of fairness is respected by colleagues and villains alike.

'The finest of all Scotland Yard series' – New York Times.

Gideon's Fire

Commander George Gideon of Scotland Yard has to deal successively with news of a mass murderer, a depraved maniac, and the deaths of a family in an arson attack on an old building south of the river. This leaves little time for the crisis developing at home ....

'Gideon of Scotland Yard emerges as one of the most real working detectives in modern fiction.... A sympathetic and believable professional policeman.' - New York Times

John Creasey

The Creepers

"The prisoner's hand was thin and bony ... And in the centre of the palm was a pinkish mark. It was the shape of a wolf's head, mouth open, fangs showing. Although it was what he had expected to see, Inspector West felt a twinge of repugnance a stab not unrelated to fear. It was the fifth time he had seen the mark of the wolf – the mark of Lobo."

A gang of cat burglars led by Lobo cause mayhem as they terrorize the city. They must be stopped, but with little in the way of evidence the police are baffled. Just how can Inspector West manage to do this in what is a race against time before more victims succumb?

"Here is an excellent novel of law enforcement officers, harried, discouraged and desperately fatigued, moving inexorably ahead under the pressure of knowledge that they must succeed to save human lives." - Cleveland Plain-Dealer

"Furiously exciting" - Chicago Tribune

"The action is fast, continuous and exciting" - San Francisco News

John Creasey

Introducing the Toff

Whilst returning home from a cricket match at his father's country home, the Honourable Richard Rollison - alias The Toff - comes across an accident which proves to be a mystery. As he delves deeper into the matter with his usual perseverance and thoroughness , murder and suspense form the backdrop to a fast moving and exciting adventure.

'The Toff has been promoted to a place of honour among amateur detectives.' – The Times Literary Supplement

Case Against Paul Raeburn

Chief Inspector Roger West has been watching and waiting for over two years – he is determined to catch Paul Raeburn out. The millionaire racketeer may have made a mistake, following the killing of a small time crook.

Can the ace detective triumph over the evil Raeburn in what are very difficult circumstances? This cannot be assumed as not eveything, it would seem, is as simple as it first appears .....

'Creasey can drive a narrative along like nobody's business ... ingenious plot ... interesting background .' - The Sunday Times

Printed in Great Britain
by Amazon